# DEATH DRAGON'S KISS

## T.K. KISER

Saint Pancratius Press

# DEATH DRAGON'S KISS

Copyright © 2017 T.K. Kiser



Saint Pancratius Press
P.O. Box 26491
Greenville, SC 29616

Ordering Information:
Quantity sales. Special discounts are available on quantity purchases by corporations, associations, and others. For details, contact the publisher at the address above.

Cover art by Ami Leshner and property of Saint Pancratius Press.

ISBN: 978-1-943835-07-2
LCCN: 2017918491

10 9 1 0 2 8 1 7

*For my grandparents*

# 1

## WEAPONS IN THE SAND

Above the crash of waves lapping onto the private shore behind the Bastion, and above the calls of gulls that soared overhead searching for a mid-day meal, swords clashed.

Bare feet marked the sand as Carine Shoemaker of North Esten and twin fifteen-year-old princes encircled one another, blades drawn. Carine wielded her awl, the same shoe-making tool that had accompanied her and the boys across the kingdom of Navafort several months prior. In her other hand was something new.

"What is this?" Carine had asked Prince David on the day he presented it to her. It was the birthday of Carine's dead father, her sweet Didda, and noticing the effect of Didda's absence on her, David excused himself from lessons with Alviar and returned ten minutes later with a balled-up undershirt and gave it to Carine.

David grinned sheepishly. His brown hair almost covered his eyes. "I didn't have paper, so I wrapped it in my shirt. Open it."

Sir Alviar, the centaur knight teaching the princes' lessons, set down his quill and made a disapproving snort, but didn't interfere. Prince Giles crossed his arms. Prince Marcel, as usual, was absent.

"I thought you planned to wait until her birthday," Giles said as Carine unrolled the shirt on the oak library table. "Besides, it belongs in the armory."

From the white cotton slipped an indigo ribbon. Carine's breath caught as the ribbon fluttered to the table.

"Don't spoil it," David said, but Carine barely heard.

The soft silk ribbon was nicer than any she had ever owned. Even Mom, who had received at least a half-dozen ribbons for birthdays and anniversaries, would marvel at the luxuriousness of the fabric.

The gift was practical too: Now that Carine's hair was growing out, she could braid it in the Navafortian tradition—which she had decided to do, like other Esteners, as a sign of patriotism during national and city-wide events. David had pestered her about the braiding protest from her past until finally she admitted that she didn't hate the kingdom but the death of her sister, for which she had blamed Navafort, the dragon Kavariel, and magic in general for many years.

"It's perfect," Carine had said, her sorrow pinched into flowing affection. "I love it." She reached forward and squeezed David into a hug, embracing the warmth of his neck and the softness of his hair as he hugged her back.

"There's more," David said, gently nudging her to see what else the gift entailed. "It's not *just* a ribbon."

Carine froze. "You mean… it's enchanted?" She looked down at the blue silk in her grasp. Besides the Manakor words they studied during lessons—which Carine carefully avoided touching with bare skin, opting to wear leather gloves instead—this was the closest she had come to magic since entering Kavariel's flame. "What does it do?"

David's ears poked out when he smiled wide. His eyes alight with enthusiasm, he said, "It took me forever to figure out. I'll show you."

Most townsfolk thought Prince Marcel was the handsomest prince, with his swooshing blonde hair and perfect teeth, and of the twins, the vast majority found Prince Giles' perfect posture and perfect grammar swoon-worthy. There were a few—whom Carine knew too well—who saw Prince David's charms, but for the most part, in her opinion, he was vastly underrated.

David closed Carine's fingers over the ribbon in her palm and stepped out of the way.

"Can't you do this outdoors?" Alviar asked, the burned side of his face making his question particularly stern. He could have read her mind; it wasn't often one had to step out of a ribbon's way. "Remember, this is a library. There are books in here."

David eased Alviar's worries and took a safe place behind Carine. From behind, he instructed, "Make a circle with your fist."

As she circled the air with the ribbon, it grew heavier and heavier until, as Carine closed the circle, she struggled to hold it. When the ribbon returned to its original position, a shield appeared where she had drawn the circle, and the ribbon welded to metal as an iron handle.

"It's for our next adventures," David had said.

Carine remembered thinking she needed no more adventures.

Carine preferred these moments, when she and the princes spent time together by themselves, just being friends. Once they had returned from the Healing Pools, it didn't take long to realize that Giles was just as withdrawn in his home environment as he was abroad, but that social David had his own group of friends, mostly girls, that he liked spending time with. But every once in a while, it was just the three of them, fencing on an Esten beach, free from danger and full of joy.

Giles' sword clanged against Carine's gifted shield.

He was tall, lean, and intentional. Giles towered over her now, barely breaking a sweat. He held out the Eldrin sword; its long reach prevented Carine from thrusting with the awl.

Giles raised the sword with both hands.

Carine turned her shield to face the sky and, sliding beneath it, rammed the shield's edge into Giles' chest.

He recoiled. His blade fell ineffectively onto the face of the shield that was her ceiling, like a shell protecting its turtle.

Carine leaped up and faced him again, repositioning the shield, but not in time.

Giles' ocean blue eyes betrayed a new certainty of victory, the same way they did five chess moves before checkmate.

Giles jabbed with the Eldrin sword and slipped it between Carine's ribs.

Carine sharply inhaled as the blade passed through her skin, stinging like a horrid bee. Giles drew it out.

Carine dropped her shield and awl on the sand and pressed her hand to her side.

No blood spilled forth.

The pain slipped away.

Besides the simple red scratch she'd find tonight where the blade had pierced, it was as though the sword had never touched her.

"I'll never get used to that," Carine said, shaking her head.

Giles smirked, tossing his hair out of his eyes and rolling his shoulders back. He was victorious.

"My turn," David said, grinning, ready with his own Eldrin sword. "Are you sure you're prepared for this, Giles?"

Giles rolled his eyes. "You always think you stand a chance against me."

Carine sat back on the sand, already forgetting where the Eldrin blade had pierced her. Only princes could fence like this: they practiced with two of the four swords in Navafort that could pierce but never wound. The swords were named after a knight who had died in battle because the first blade of its kind—enchanted by Kavariel during Festival— had failed to wound his adversary. Due to their rarity and the danger of mixing them up with unenchanted swords, these blades were used only at the annual sword-fighting competitions, which would start tomorrow. They could also be acquired, it turned out, by persuasive princes who sought them for amusement and sport.

Sweat collected at David's hairline and rolled down the side of his face. He lunged toward his fraternal twin, raising his sword and bringing it down in such a way that Giles' smile disappeared until he lifted his sword to defend himself.

The royal twins were better matched now. Giles was stronger and more precise with his blade, but David had been practicing every day since Prince Marcel got the credit for healing Kavariel. Most days, Carine was right there with him, whether in the arena, on the beach, or sneaking in some practice with wooden sticks in David's room or the library. She was getting better, especially with her shield, but when her skills did not challenge him enough, David also practiced with Alviar and other knights, and—when Carine or David could find him—with Giles, who often disappeared to work on private research projects.

"I want…" David had panted last week when they were practicing in the same arena where the true competitions would be, "…him to notice." *Him* was His Majesty King Marcel, David's grandfather, the only father-figure the twins had ever known. Unfortunately for them, King Marcel exclusively cared for his namesake, the eldest and heir apparent, Prince Marcel.

It was Marcel who got credit for the return of the protective flame. It was Marcel whom their grandfather pulled from lessons for special royal conferences and speeches. It was only Marcel whom the king ever noticed at the dining table or acknowledged with a proud lift of his royal chin.

Carine had been present for one of these occasions. By a miracle of influence, David had convinced the king's advisor to let Carine sit at the end of the feast table, with forty or fifty guests, to celebrate His Majesty's coronation anniversary last month. At the height of the meal, the king lifted his goblet and raised a toast to the kingdom and the Marcel line. Seated at the king's right hand, Prince Marcel lifted his glass as well; the king swelled with pride, lifted his chin, and recited for everyone the prized prince's accolades, including three or four items that in fact the twins had accomplished instead. David hardly touched the rest of his meal, and the next morning was out with his sword earlier than ever.

Even today, the twins were relegated to the shore outside the Bastion walls, but Prince Marcel was allowed to practice in the arena, flanked by a dozen servants and watched by King Marcel himself.

David's only hope to receive his grandfather's approval was tomorrow at the tournament, and Carine had volunteered to watch the king's expression for him.

Giles deflected David's attack, but not without a crease in his forehead that betrayed his concentration. Giles swung, sword slicing through the salty breeze.

David ducked and slashed back.

Light on his feet, Giles parried the blow. Striking back from above, he sliced through David's shoulder with a grin.

David fell, panting, his Eldrin blade landing in the sand beside him.

Carine stared with wide eyes, frozen, as Giles pulled the metal from David's flesh. The breeze chilled her bones as she remembered the last time she had seen Giles stab someone with a sword. Not knowing Firebrand's heir was her father, Giles had plunged his sword into Didda's chest, leading to his death.

Carine pushed the memory from her mind, breathing on her shield's handle and feeling it lighten as it melted back into a simple ribbon. She hadn't told Giles that he had met her dead father, let alone that he had harmed him. She wanted to share that secret with her friend, but there was something nice about Giles not knowing. He didn't ooze sympathy like David did when she just wanted to forget, and he couldn't judge the mistakes her father had made in his final days. This distance was a sweet relief, though at the cost, perhaps, of a deeper truthfulness between them.

David stretched back over the chilly sand granules, hands over his head, and mused to his brother, "Aron's not as good as you. I can still beat him tomorrow."

Giles clipped his enchanted sword back into its special leather sheath. "Yes, but he doesn't fight like menfolk."

"Doesn't matter," said a chipper female voice from the dunes. Carine groaned inside. She had almost managed to forget these girls were here. "Prince David will still take the victory."

# 2

## INCLUSION

Sophie's long, light brown hair was braided with sky blue ribbons that fluttered in the breeze. She rested on her elbows on the blanket the nobles' daughters had brought to protect their white and yellow dresses from the sand. Two others reclined with her, gossiping, watching the practice, and waiting for David to finish today's fencing so they could chat and dine with the middle prince.

There were an additional two that liked to hang around, but today, it seemed they had fancied to take a walk down the shoreline, and were now on their way back, leaning their heads close to each other like they were whispering and giggling over shared secrets. This, Carine had found, was the primary reason any of them went on walks.

Prince David raised his fist in response to Sophie's encouragement, leaping to his feet. "Where are Millie and Elizabeth?"

Sophie smiled and told him.

Carine rolled her eyes. When she first learned that there were others in the twins' social circle, Carine had a flicker of sweet hope: She hadn't had a female friend since her sister died, and perhaps these five would be the answer to a wish.

At first, they were all honey: "I'm Sophie," Sophie had said with a sparkling, demure smile. They introduced themselves one by one, eyes dancing as they looked at the unknown girl who had made the short invitation list to a small dinner in the Dining Hall with the twins. Their eyes drifted down to her best outfit, which no doubt was drab by their standards. Carine watched their smiles politely freeze in place so they wouldn't accidentally reveal their disgust.

"How did you meet their highnesses? Are you a diplomat's daughter? Are you from another kingdom?" they asked, noting her short hair and lack of lip stain. All these ideas enchanted them, and perhaps, if Carine was the type of person to do so, she would have let them believe their fantasies.

Instead, she evaded the question about meeting the princes, and told the girls instead that no, she lived in Esten.

"Are you new? Did you just move here? Surely we would have seen you before if you hadn't. What lane do you live on? Perhaps we should bring your family a welcome basket!" the girls said. "Are you by the entry gates? I should introduce you to my cousins. Much of my family lives there."

"I'm from North Esten," Carine answered. The room went silent.

"North Esten?" said one of the girls, confused.

"She means the Grunge," Millie said, her voice low. Carine clenched her teeth. The silence grew thick and uncomfortable.

It was Sophie that broke through the awkwardness. "Well...Prince David is so *nice*, isn't he? He's very inclusive."

"Yes," agreed the girls.

"Wouldn't turn away anyone."

After that, she did her best to avoid them, which became somewhat easier as the girls realized over time that Carine wasn't a one-time pity invite. They kept their distance, as did she, and tolerated Carine's faded garments and the impropriety of her participation in fencing practice. At times that seemed random to Carine, they lashed out, cruelly answering a question with "go ask the Naga," meaning, "go ask the part-man, part-snake if you care so much, and we don't mind if you get eaten while you're at it." At other times, they sidled up to her, interested—it turned out—in drama.

"So… Are you and his highness Prince David… together?" Sophie asked one day, violating their protocol of avoidance.

"No," Carine said, feeling embarrassed and offended at once. She stifled the urge to tell her off with that same mean phrase that Sophie had used on her.

Sophie smiled. "Good. Millie has a crush on him, and we all just wanted to know." This was the reason Sophie took such delight in David taking notice of Millie and Elizabeth's absence. Sophie would report to Millie later on, and the girls would spend hours analyzing.

Turned out their romantic interests in David weren't without encouragement: Sophie had been David's first kiss, even though they never kissed again. Apparently, for a short while, David had courted a few other girls that used to be part of the friend group. For the most part, Mom thought David must be oblivious to the girls' affection, but deep down, Carine suspected he liked the attention and basked in it.

At any moment, Carine was sure, David would tell her he was going to ask Millie out.

To an extent, she craved this. Such an intention was only shared with one's closest friends, and hearing this would be confirmation that she counted among them. However, she also dreaded such a moment. Since Carine was a girl, if David fancied any other girl, that would mean he liked her more than Carine. It would mean they would share intimate thoughts, and that Carine would be stuck on the sidelines with Giles, her relationship with David growing fainter and fainter.

Sometimes she felt that her time with David was like a small diamond discovered on a sparkling beach. Try as she might to keep it in her palm, one breeze or slight misstep would knock the diamond into the sandy expanse, never to be found again.

Carine swallowed a sigh as Millie and Elizabeth approached.

"What does our soon-to-be fencing champion think about this morning's...events?" Millie asked David with intrigue in her eyes, twisting a slender braid around her finger.

"We're not supposed to talk about that," Millie's younger sister hissed. She was sitting on the dune with Sophie; Carine could never remember her name.

"Oh relax." Millie leaned close to the twins. "Your *highnesses* are sure to know what happened on my street this morning to my neighbor."

David shot a questioning glance at Giles, who shrugged. "I only just found out before practice."

"Found out what?" David asked.

"My neighbor was executed this morning. In his home," Millie said, as if exposing a fashion faux-pas. "His wife was all distressed about it." The girl's voice hushed lower, and with the crashing of the rising tide, Carine had to strain to hear her. "Somebody found out that he had *it*."

"Had what?" Carine asked. What possession could someone possibly own that would make killing him without trial necessary?

"The *mark*," the girl hissed. "The black mark on his skin from the stories. The *Death Dragon's Kiss*."

"Ha!" David laughed, his mirth forced. "Yeah right." His smile faded as a nod from Giles confirmed Millie's story.

Carine trembled. She had heard tales of the death dragon. His name was Uriel, and he wasn't at all like the ash dragon Kavariel. Kavariel, like most of the other beasts, protected a certain region of the world. He was armed with scales and fire, and came to Esten bearing a mixed bag of blessings and punishments.

But the death dragon, Uriel, neither wore scales nor breathed fire. It was said that the death dragon was like smoke. He descended upon the starving and ill and ripped their souls from their failing flesh. If you could see him with your eyes, you were already dead.

"The Death Dragon's Kiss?" David said. "In Esten?"

The mark Mille had mentioned was a black, inky stain that Carine had only ever heard about in stories, and thank the flames had never seen in real life. It was said that the stain was a kiss from Uriel, a sign that he would soon be back for his prey. No matter how hard you washed, you could never scrub the kiss away, and no matter how fast you ran, you could never outpace your doom.

In Navafort, as well as other kingdoms, the law was clear: anyone found with the Death Dragon's Kiss was to be immediately executed.

Swift, complete eradication was critical, for there had never been a city marked by the Death Dragon's Kiss that hadn't completely been destroyed. Uriel, descending on his victim, would kiss and devour the rest of the city too. All that would be discovered, days later, would be hundreds or thousands of bodies and a city that once had been.

"Can you imagine if they hadn't found him out?" Sophie said, standing now with her hand on her hip. "We'd all be dead."

"Good thing they got to him first," said Millie. "Don't you think so, Carine?" Comments like these made Carine suspect they had now heard the rumors about her family's strange Festival tradition.

"Yeah," she echoed, not sure which she feared more: a kingdom that killed its citizen for bearing a mark he hadn't sought to acquire, or the chance that the death dragon would return to Esten anyway. "Good thing."

# 3

## ROYAL SEATS

The next day, the crowd screamed with delight as victorious Prince Marcel flipped his blonde hair across his sweaty forehead and raised his arms. He beamed in the middle of the sandy arena, as a salty autumn breeze lifted the Navafortian pennants that flapped above the fourth level of seats.

Carine peered into the arena from a gap between the stands, her leather-gloved hands shaking more than she'd expected.

King Marcel, having watched Prince Marcel's match from his chair, lifted his chin slightly, and gave the littlest hint of a smile.

That. That was what David was dying for. That was the look he had been talking about for weeks. That was why, when they were sweaty and exhausted, David pressed for fifteen more minutes of practice. It was why he dropped to do pushups anytime it rained and they couldn't go outside. It was why, probably, he was playing up his confidence now.

"How do I look?" came David's bright, easy voice.

Carine turned.

David looked regal and victorious already, and he hadn't yet stepped onto the sand. He was wearing a velvet crimson cape over a thick, embroidered fighting vest. His hair was clean and a little rugged and his smile was wide. His arms were spread out to show off his outfit, which—best of all—featured the boots that Carine had engraved for him. She had spent three weeks drawing Kavariel's flame and other highlights from their adventure together. He was magnificent.

But he wasn't asking her.

"Soot and ash!"

"You'll beat him for sure."

His friends oohed around him, checking to make sure that his sleeves were rolled down and his cape was in place.

Carine tried to make eye contact, but David was showing off his helmet.

A sinking regret settled over her soul. She wished now she hadn't offered to watch for King Marcel's expression. At first, it had felt like an opportunity to help David in a special way. But today it seemed more like a recipe to disappoint him: if David lost, he would receive no sign of affection from the king. If David won but the king did not convey the desired validation, Carine would be responsible for bearing the disastrous news.

Suddenly Carine's heart lifted; David made eye contact and jogged over to her, carrying his helmet under his arm. Of all the girls around him, he had specifically sought her out.

"You'll do great," she said, surprised as David took her shoulders in his hands.

"Thanks," he said distractedly as he checked the arena. "Soot and ash, he's already on." Out on the arena's sand,

David's opponent, Sir Aron, was ready for battle. Carine gulped. Aron was a centaur, one of the folk gifted with mighty strength, but that didn't seem to bother David. He had prepared for this. "Listen, I got you a spot where you can see better."

He took her gloved hand and raced—a bit fast—around the raised seats. Within a minute, Carine was sitting next to Prince Giles. Giles, at ease in his full royal garb, wore his indigo cape and slender, shining sword the same way she wore her old surcoat or her father's boots. His tipped-up nose elongated his neck, but his thin smile greeting told Carine that she was allowed to be present, that he found her acceptable. Classic Giles. Carine smiled.

David looked at the king from his seat, even as the crowd was cheering for him. "You can see grandfather perfectly from here."

King Marcel was a grumpy man with deep lines in the sagging skin around his frown and under his eyes. He tended to hunch when he stood, but seated, his back was flat against the throne, muscles tensed in his neck and arms as though bracing himself.

His golden crown shone brightly in the sun. It had been polished for today's event, so it gleamed in all its gold and ruby splendor. The crown's peaks were like the torches around the kingdom. And in true Navafort fashion, the rubies were nested on the base between embossed dragon designs.

David's deep brown eyes drew Carine's attention. "I'm counting on you."

His gaze broke at the shouts of the crowd. "Prince Da-vid!" the folk shouted.

David looked up and waved. Then, with a breath, he slid on his helmet. The metallic tail of an embossed dragon covered the bridge of his nose. Hands balled in fists, he marched onto the sand.

# 4

## GREAT MARCEL

Carine's heart pounded.

Prince David, despite his regal attire and the strength he had gained through practice, was short and skinny compared to the monstrous centaur knight beside him. Unlike Alviar's white gleaming coat, Sir Aron's was brown with black spots on his flank that gave Carine a small shudder; she couldn't shake Millie's ominous gossip about the Death Dragon's Kiss. Fortunately, Carine had seen Sir Aron before, and these spots had been his from birth.

David straightened his neck, as if sensing the disparity and determined to prove himself superior. He didn't dare focus his eyes on any of the crowd members, but his face was turned solidly to Carine's left, where, a few seats away, sat His Majesty King Marcel, the queen, and the attendants. With the curve of the arena, Carine could see the king easily.

"Your Majesty," proclaimed the king's advisor from the sand. The king's advisor was a short man with curling brown hair and an upturned nose. His nose turned up even higher today, the day of his greatest public appearance since he served as the voice of the king for the tournament. He was the announcer and the referee. The little man nodded dramatically to the contestants. "I present to you for the next competition Sir Aron and…His Hi-i-i-ghness…Prince Da-a-avid!"

The crowd cheered.

The king's knobby fingers were curled over the chair's arm rests. He nodded grumpily, but if Carine hadn't been looking closely, she wouldn't have registered any motion from the king at all. His eyes were milky and strange.

The advisor—who, naturally, could be overruled at any moment by the king—unsheathed the first Eldrin sword. Its long, silver blade glimmered.

An assistant set a caged rabbit at the advisor's feet, and promptly the blade was thrust into the creature's back.

The white creature shuddered, but when the blade was drawn out clean, the rabbit carried on living.

This tradition was faithfully kept before each competition, because in the rule of the previous King Marcel, one particularly competitive knight had switched the enchanted sword out for a normal, lethal one.

Bowing, the referee offered the sword to Prince David with both hands.

The girls, somewhere in the stadium, shrieked with delight. David looked up and beamed. The veil of his formality fell away, and all that was left was sweet David, Carine's closest friend who just needed to know he was loved.

David's mother, the queen, sat next to the king in a sky-blue gown. Technically the queen was only a princess. She wasn't the king's wife, but rather his daughter-in-law. However, the true queen had long been dead by the time the twins' father died, and the people began to call the twin's mother the queen instead. The honor stuck, and now she attended formal regal events with a dedication she didn't show her sons.

The queen was tall. She wore short curly blonde wigs to cover her greying hair. Carine hardly ever saw her—except at events like these—and the twins didn't like to talk about her much, but whenever Carine did see her, she was always wearing an elegant gown and was pinching her lips together in a way that made her face look too tight. She had gorgeous blue eyes that she must have passed down to Giles, and liked to bat her long, dark eyelashes at whichever suitor was sitting beside her that week or month.

Today, her suitor of choice looked rather southern, perhaps from an island kingdom. Ilmaria, maybe? He looked just as snooty and rich as David described the suitors his mother chose.

Carine wished that her own care for David could be enough for him. Carine was watching King Marcel closely now, and there was something wrong about him—more so than usual. Her stomach clenched.

The king's advisor bowed low and exited the ring. "Begin!"

The Eldrin swords clashed.

"Does His Majesty look alright to you?" Carine asked Giles, careful to use all the proper formalities in case anyone overheard. If they were chatting on the shore or in the library, she might just say "your grandfather," though usually she preferred "King Marcel."

"He always looks grumpy," Giles said matter-of-factly, eyes glued to the competition. He cringed as David made a misstep, but his twin in the ring quickly recovered.

Carine turned back to the king. His wrinkled fingers, covered in oversized rings, gripped the arms of the chair. His golden crown angled slightly over his forehead like a brow. His permanent frown drooped more than usual.

The only motion he made, the only flicker of anything inside, was the slow lifting of his handkerchief.

He pressed the folded white handkerchief to his lips. His eyes didn't even track the moving competitors; he would have looked bored, if he didn't look…ill.

"Lift your chin," she whispered, watching the king.

Giles clicked his tongue. "David should have struck just then. His opponent was vulnerable."

"Come on," Carine hissed like a wish. "Lift your chin."

Instead, King Marcel took a labored breath and let the handkerchief drop from his lips. The white fabric was beautiful, and at this short distance Carine could even see the intricate flower pattern in the corner of the cloth.

But that wasn't what made her recoil. The needlework wasn't what put the sour taste in Carine's mouth: there was a gel, a black shiny phlegm in the center of the king's cloth with dark speckles all around it.

Disgust turned to terror. Coughing up black phlegm wasn't just repulsive; it was a sign of the Kiss.

The crowd cheered. Someone had won, but Carine couldn't muster the strength to turn her head.

All she could see was the dark spot in the king's handkerchief. Somewhere on his skin would be the dark mark that would call the dragon to Esten to feed.

Suddenly things were happening, but Carine could hardly take it in. It was as if everything blurred together and she was watching from far away. A dull ringing sounded in her ears as her face and hands clammed up.

The advisor was back on the sand lifting someone's hand. He was lifting David's hand. David was smiling. He was looking at Carine, and then he was looking at other people.

His Majesty King Marcel didn't lift his chin.

He didn't move at all, except he let his head fall back against the throne, and expelled one final breath.

"Your Majesty?" Carine heard someone say. The king's open eyes glazed over. They didn't close; they didn't blink. "Your Majesty!"

The handkerchief dropped from the king's lifeless hand.

**5**

# DEATH DRAGON'S KISS

Carine shivered, checking the skies for the invisible death dragon Uriel, even knowing she couldn't see him if he were there. Her last experience of the ash dragon Kavariel was breathtaking, but the death dragon never visited a place to deliver a flame or breathe Manakor words onto city walls. Carine recalled with horror an illustration of what the death dragon would look like were he visible: made of smoke, smiting his victims by charging like wind through their chests, taking their souls with him.

The king's advisor fruitlessly checked for a pulse in His Majesty's wrist and neck. A confirmation announcement was made that he was in fact dead, and as though the servants and advisors were in retreat, the body was quickly ushered off. Four servants carried the dead king on the throne while the queen and three princes followed after.

David seemed to have lost all sense of place. His head hung heavy as he breathed slowly through his mouth, following Prince Marcel's steps as though ropes were linked to his feet. His eyes stared past the sand that his boots grazed over. A pang hit Carine's heart. King Marcel was the closest figure David had to a father. She knew what this was like.

Giles stood and left his seat by Carine. He walked beside his twin, though the death did not affect his posture. His lips were tight, and he knit his eyebrows. His fierce blue eyes revealed that his thoughts weren't here either, but rather processing.

Carine was processing too, a calculation that was quickly boiling into anger.

King Marcel had borne the Death Dragon's Kiss. The tar cough, said the tales, was a last-chance sign of the Kiss after the folk had already been marked for death. King Marcel had to have seen the mark on his skin. He had to have known for days and days.

The people, at first too shocked to speak, couldn't stop chattering. Some of them hummed a reverent battle hymn for the king, but most were talking about Prince Marcel.

Carine's teeth clenched as she realized that the late king had probably already had the curse when he sentenced the cursed man on Millie's street to die. The cowardly king hadn't had the courage to reveal his own affliction, even if it meant endangering his people.

The curse of the other man hadn't been permitted to come to fruition. Folk were able to execute him before the death dragon did. This was supposed to keep the death dragon from coming at all. Now, however, it was the Death Dragon's Kiss that ended His Majesty King Marcel's life. Invisible to the eye, the death dragon Uriel was here in Esten, and the tales clearly told that he wouldn't leave until he had raked all souls from their bodily homes. A man with the mark had died. It was inevitable now.

Carine squeezed her eyes shut as her head pounded. A year ago, Carine would have run into her house, locked the door, and boarded up the windows. But as her best friends disappeared in a line to the Bastion, and as she caught sight of Mom, surprisingly braided and well dressed, in the crowd, Carine took a breath.

A chill went down her spine as she looked into the empty sky. The death dragon was not visible like other dragons, but he inflicted worse harms just as real.

Stepping over to the area where the royals had sat, Carine knelt, her gloves sifting over the surface of the sand.

There, partially covered when the throne was moved, was the white handkerchief, with the thick black splotch crusted in sand.

Careful not to touch the tar even with the fabric of her glove, she picked up the kerchief, folded it the other way, and tucked it into her pocket.

However hard it might be to tell them right now, the princes had to know that King Marcel hadn't died by accident, and the beast that killed him was coming for everyone else.

# 6

## MERE LEGEND

Carine barely made it through the castle gate. The servants had gotten used to letting her through the big double doors, but today, after having seen the king's body minutes before, they hesitated. Carine didn't give them a chance to stop her.

The handkerchief, though light in weight, felt like a boulder in her pocket. Carine couldn't forget its ominous stain even as she pushed through the hallway past knights with helmets in their hands and servants who were only now relaying hearsay of the day's events. Mom had seen her run off, confused, but Carine tried to tell her through a glance to trust her.

Her mission came to a crashing halt, however, at the thick oak doors that closed off the Great Hall. In her months in the Bastion, Carine had never seen these doors shut, not once, until now.

Her gloved fist hit the door. "David," she almost said, to get their attention, but a knight stopped her. He took one look at her best dress and concluded that she was a North Estener, a nobody from the Grunge.

"How dare you disturb their majesties' mourning?" he said.

She took a breath. "I have an urgent message for the princes."

"That you're there for them?" he mocked. "You're just like my niece, drooling after the princes. They rank above you, and they are in mourning."

She shut her eyes. "It's urgent."

"Who let you in here?"

"Please."

"The girl's with me," said a voice. Carine turned around. Alviar, with his burned face and long white hair stood tall on his centaur legs. His flank was decorated with centaur jewelry, a string of indigo beads that encircled his middle horizontally.

Alviar was a good teacher, though strict. He hadn't had to accept her into lessons with the princes, and he didn't have to tolerate her endless questions about Manakor. Nevertheless, he did.

Alviar had challenged her black and white childhood beliefs about dragons back on the ship, and unlike the stark contrast between his black eyebrow and shirts and white coat and hair, Alviar introduced Carine to a more nuanced understanding of the universe.

His arms were crossed, and the message was received.

The knight stepped out of the way.

"Shoemaker, what are you doing here? This isn't a social time." Alviar's aging eyes betrayed sympathy, a desire to believe that she had good intentions. It was surprising.

Despite their differences, Alviar and Carine had two very important similarities: both cared for the twins, and both of them had heard their names called in the dragon Kavariel's flame.

Carine had only dared to speak of her experience in the flame once with Sir Alviar. It was late one night when she and the twins had been struggling with the concept of destiny as used in the Manakor language and writings.

"I think I understand what you mean," David had said. He set down the feather pen he'd been mindlessly sweeping against his cheek. "When we healed the dragon, we heard our names."

"We?" Alviar said, scanning their eyes.

Giles raised an eyebrow, a motion he sometimes used instead of shrugging. "I wasn't in the flame with them. I was busy defeating our adversary."

Carine clenched her teeth and diverted her attention from what "defeating our adversary" meant for her family.

"You were there too? In the flame?" Alviar asked.

Carine nodded.

"But how were you not burned?" he said, wonder and envy betraying themselves in his half-burned face.

"The dragon's magic, I guess," David said, only a part-lie, to cover up Carine's power. Technically even her Gift of Calling was dragon's magic. It came from dragon's blood in her veins.

"And you heard your names like I did?"

Carine nodded.

She expected Alviar to say how he wished the dragon had spared his face as well. Instead, he said, "Remember that. Remember your names, for memory is your compass. Those who forget lose themselves."

He turned back to the book to go on to the next piece of information for them, but stopped himself. "Actually, memory is important, but not enough to breathe life into a weary soul. I used to think it was." Alviar touched his folded, burned cheek. "In dark moments I tried and failed to rekindle the striking beauty of that moment when Kavariel burned me. The memory left me as dry as brush rolling through a desert."

"What instead, then?" Giles asked. "If memory doesn't help you."

"Ask," Alviar answered. "Hope. *Wish.* Aid will come."

Now, a shiver went up Carine's spine. "I need to speak with the princes."

"Why?" Despite their history, Alviar's job was still to train and defend the princes, even if that meant defending them from one who might interrupt their grieving.

Inhaling sharply, Carine retrieved the handkerchief from her pocket. She unfolded it and presented it with both hands.

Alviar clopped back. The black tar drained the color from his face. "You?" There was a horror in his expression, and Carine realized he thought she was the one with the Kiss.

But then he noticed the royal embroidery. His expression hardened.

"I see," he said, folding the kerchief and putting it in his pocket. "I will notify the princes at once." He stepped forward to enter the Great Hall. "Thank you."

"Alviar," Carine said, reaching out. A shiver ran through her. "This means..." she lowered her voice. She couldn't say out loud that Esten would be wiped out. "Alviar…what are we going to do? Do we run? Can we fight? I need to protect my mom. She's…she's the only family I have left."

Alviar put his heavy hand on Carine's shoulder. "Even the death dragon is obedient to the Etherrealm. There is good in that. There is hope in that."

"But Kavariel was an obedient dragon. He killed my sister."

Alviar nodded. "Hope first. Do you understand?"

Carine wanted to say no, but she nodded.

"We know little of this supposed curse. The only source we have is hearsay and legend."

"…Legends that say that if someone with the Death Dragon's Kiss dies, then the whole city will be wiped out."

"Patience. We have much to learn. I will first confirm that the black mark exists on the king's corpse. Then, Prince Marcel will make a plan."

"Prince Marcel? But he's…" Lazy. Self-centered. Unprepared to be king.

"…The heir, Shoemaker." Alviar sighed. "At his best, he has charm and is a good fighter, and his best is what the people will see."

"What about my mom?" Carine said.

Alviar lifted his chin. "You are a good student, Shoemaker, and you have proven yourself valuable to Navafort."

"So…will you protect my mother?"

He closed his eyes. "I will. I will see to it personally."

A weight lifted in Carine's heart. "Thank you. You don't know how much this—."

"I need your word, Carine, that you will return the favor when I ask."

Carine nodded. "You have it."

"Very well. Go. Bring your mother to the Bastion. I will share the news with the princes. And hurry. We may not have much time."

# 7

## CONTAGION

Mom didn't need much urging. She stuffed a bag with necessities as Carine undressed behind the quilt.

Carefully, very thoroughly, Carine checked her arms and legs and every inch of her body for the smallest dark speck.

If King Marcel had been marked by the death dragon, she could be too.

But between her toes was nothing but sock lint, and Mom verified that no mark lurked behind her ears.

With a sigh of relief, Carine was ready to pack. She wasn't marked, but that didn't mean she was safe.

Carine changed into her normal fall clothes: long sleeved white undergown, pink surcoat, engraved boots, and leather gloves to protect her skin from accidentally making contact with Manakor.

To touch a written word of the Manakor language would be to use the Gift of Calling she had inherited from her father. Touching the language was called pronunciation, because—since she had the Gift—her soul would "speak" Manakor as purely as the nine obedient dragons did. This power, which her granddad Jon called "wishing," had saved her life more than once, and ultimately saved the dragon Kavariel and all of Navafort.

She didn't dare touch the word again. Even the thought of using the Gift of Calling was too much. The last time she'd done so—despite saving Navafort—her father had died. It had been painful to wish and even more painful to lose him. There was nothing worth going through that again, and nothing worth risking ending up as distorted as Didda was in his final days.

She and David talked about wishing sometimes. They talked about Kavariel and what he had looked like. David asked her when she might use her powers again. Carine didn't hate magic in general like she had before. But she didn't care for pronunciation, which hurt and wasn't certain to have the desired effect.

And she certainly would never impose her own will on a Manakor word, usually evidenced by speaking it out loud. Her granddad, in his journal, called this mispronunciation "compulsion." His notes warned of its dangers, but Carine didn't need that reminder. She would never compel. She would never pervert her Gift the way Didda had done. She'd seen what it did to him. She'd seen the damage it caused.

Carine fastened the narrow leather belt around her waist. In her pocket was a set of wishstones and her awl, which had served her in the past as a makeshift weapon.

Now that Carine had her enchanted ribbon-shield, which she tied around the end of her short braid, she felt less comfortable than when she had hidden away in the shoe shop with her family. It was as though now that she had a shield on hand, she was more likely to need it. With a shiver, she pictured the death dragon, invisible to her eye, ripping out King Marcel's soul and leaving his body dead and limp in his chair.

"Where will Alviar send us?" Mom asked, stuffing a comb and a pair of socks into her pack.

"I don't know yet." Carine's heart thudded. She leaned her forehead against the cold window glass and looked up at the sky. In years past she had feared that Kavariel might show up suddenly outside the period of Festival. Today, she searched the skies for a creature she knew her bare eyes wouldn't catch. The death dragon always came to those cities where a marked one died. He always destroyed. He always left bare.

At least, that's what the stories said.

"I'll be outside," Carine said, antsy. She shut the door behind her as the breezy afternoon caught her breath. Birds flitted from rooftop to rooftop as neighbors told of the morning's events. Folk had mostly returned from the competition by now, but the king's death was still breaking news.

Little did they know the cause.

Her boots tapped the cobblestone as she waited for Mom. It was time to leave Esten or hide in the Bastion.

Carine's heart stopped, then raced into double-time: across the street, her neighbors—the three who had tormented her for years—were shouting at each other.

Giselle, the tall girl with the stringy black hair, had her arm across her doorway to block her cousin from entry. "Not in my house, you don't. I don't want the death dragon coming here!"

Her cousin gritted his teeth. "What would you have me do, huh? You want them to find out about me? Execute me?" The last question was thick in his mouth. It was then that Carine registered the cause of their fight: there was an ink-black streak across his cheek.

He shoved past her. "I'm going inside."

Before he could make good on his promise, Giselle drew back her arm and slammed her fist into his eye.

The marked boy staggered back.

The girl's brother, Elias, in defense of his leader, pulled her down by the shoulder and punched her in the face.

"Not me, you idiot," she said as Elias got his footing and clenched his fists. "He's the one with the…"

Giselle pointed at her cousin and stopped mid-sentence. Her arm froze, suspended in space as she noticed—and Carine and the boys noticed—the inky splotch across her knuckles.

The second boy stared at his own right hand. It too had stained.

Carine was frozen still. She was staring, but couldn't help it.

Both brother and sister had the mark on their knuckles, which had made contact with a marked one. When they punched each other, the kiss spread to the first point of contact.

Carine understood: the curse was contagious.

"What are you staring at?" Giselle snapped, meeting Carine's gaze.

"She knows," said Elias. His eyes cut to Carine.

Carine clenched her jaw.

"Who cares? She's just a shoemaker," said the cousin.

Giselle thumped his forehead. "She's friends with the princes, you idiot. She'll tell them, and we'll be executed."

"There's only one way she won't tell about our marks," said Giselle, stepping forward. "If she has one too."

"Mom?" Carine called toward the door, skirting into a run as the trio charged. Terror surged through her like lightning, but just as she came to the end of the street, Carine stopped in her tracks.

To go through this again with these three, after how they had avoided her when they realized she was friends with royalty, was beyond irritating. If only they knew the power she had. If only they knew that with a word she could destroy them. If only they had the slightest inkling of her power, they wouldn't approach her. They wouldn't bother her. They wouldn't threaten her.

She turned to face them, fingers twitching over her pocket, and watched them come. She had been tempted before to compel, to speak aloud the Manakor words that would make real her desires, but in previous moments she had overcome the longing. Now, with these three tiresome neighbors threatening her life to save themselves, she recalled useful Manakor words she'd studied in Alviar's lessons. She could taste the power on her tongue.

But just as the sick thought took hold, her sweet mother left their little shoe shop and closed the door behind her, looking around for her daughter.

In that moment, Carine knew she could not bring herself to compel with her power. She refused to do what Didda had done.

Carine pushed the Etherrealm's language from her mind, and instead reached for her ribbon.

The three were only steps away, but far enough for Carine to extend her arm as her hair billowed out behind her. She made a circle in the air, and the ribbon became a heavy shield.

The trio stopped.

One approached: tall Elias, the third one to get infected. Careful to hit him where she knew he'd survive, Carine turned her shield to the side and slammed the edge into his chest. The boy buckled over his middle and dropped, arms wrapped around his stomach. The other two stood still.

"Go home," Carine said, as Mom approached, eyes wide, from behind. "I won't tell them about you." They didn't move. "Go home," she repeated, and at that, the boy picked himself up and followed the others as they darted home.

# 8

## THE NINTH

"My people," Prince Marcel proclaimed, standing on the repaired balcony that Didda had destroyed months prior. He had opened the doors to the balcony as Mom and Carine pushed their way through the assemblage of folk gathering in Bastion Park.

His long blonde hair was shiny. His mouth was wide, his chin was raised, and his posture was easy but confident. His voice projected well over the large park, and his purple cloak looked seemly over softer, more formal clothes than the shiny armor he had donned earlier for the tournament.

"…Today is a day we mourn the loss of my grandfather, His Majesty King Marcel…"

Prince Marcel had the ease that an engrained belief of superiority puts in you. His redeeming quality—if it could redeem—was his charm, which he flexed to its full advantage for this hasty coronation.

Behind the prince stood the king's advisor. He held a purple pillow with the king's now-silver crown on top of it. This was an enchanted feature of Navafort's crown: it turned silver when not on the head of the king.

Mom reached out for Carine's wrist, as she looked up to watch.

"...I am advised we must act quickly. Therefore, the remainder of the tournament is cancelled. There will be no great coronation ceremony..."

Prince Marcel's words were regal and well-delivered. However, even through his smile, Carine detected reluctance, as though this speech were a task someone was making him carry out.

To a certain extent, Carine felt sorry for him. He was in his late teens, and his heart was elsewhere. For a while Carine had blamed him for his tendency to nap and skip lessons, skating by on the late king's favor. But David and Giles told her, one day when she mentioned something about his naps, that shortly before Selius the Heartless One came to Esten months ago, Prince Marcel had been in love.

The late king disapproved of the match, and sent the girl, Evelline, away, to an undisclosed location, where the prince could never follow her. Prince Marcel had been in "mourning" on the boat when Carine first met him, and perhaps this was what led him to the crown with such a heavy heart.

Prince Marcel's attire jingled as he knelt on one knee.

The king's blonde advisor lifted the silver crown over the prince's head. "Do you accept this crown and the rule of Navafort? Do you accept responsibility for this kingdom and its wellbeing?"

He responded in monotone. "I do."

With that, the crown landed on his head. In a swirl of enchantment, the silver flourished into gold, a sign it was worn by its rightful heir.

"Behold," proclaimed the advisor, "His Majesty King Marcel of Navafort, the ninth!"

The crowd bowed and cheered at once.

Prince—*King*—Marcel stood and lifted his arms.

"Glory to the Great Marcels! Glory to the Great Marcels!"

Carine shivered. The "great" King Marcel had a kingdom to protect.

# 9

## CURSE

The castle guards wouldn't let Carine through. Even after seeing her earlier that day, they had concluded that the only ones allowed through the door were members of the royal court.

"You don't understand," Carine was saying, as Mom warily searched the skies for the death dragon. "We have to get in. Sir Alviar promised…"

"Young Shoemaker," the bright white and ink-black centaur called, clopping to the castle doors. Alviar stopped with an assured step in his hooves at the gate. He was wearing a red stole for mourning. Carine realized that she should have worn red too, though the closest garments she had to that color were faded pink. "There you are." He gestured wide to welcome them inside. "Hello, Helen, isn't it?"

"Yes, Sir Alviar," Mom said, clasping his hand in hers. They had only met once or twice, but whenever Carine mentioned tutoring, Mom was overwhelmed by the generosity of the castle to bring a North Estener—her daughter— into lessons. "I can't thank you enough. For teaching my daughter, for making sure we have a place to go." Carine hadn't told Mom about the deal Carine had made to help

Alviar when he asked for it, but that didn't seem relevant now, since their first order of business was to survive.

Alviar nodded. "I can only do my best, madam. This way."

The Bastion's halls flurried with activity. A tremor of nerves flitted through the rooms and among the glances of servants bustling to and fro. Prince—King—Marcel could compete fairly well in swordplay; he could attract the attention of young women who found him handsome; but he was no leader, despite Alviar's defense of him.

Carine drew in breath. Worse than the twins' brother as king would be an impending visit by the beast of doom. "About his late majesty..." Carine ventured, lowering her voice as they turned a corner to a hallway where the servants stood still and could be listening. "Did you find out about...?"

Alviar nodded briskly, his blue eyes instructing her to stop speaking lest they be overheard as they came to a halt at the doors of the Great Hall. He knocked, then clopped back.

Alviar leaned toward Carine, voice low. Mom leaned in to hear. Despite the newness of the castle's interior to her, she had not forgotten the threat that had propelled her from her home. "Unfortunately, young Shoemaker, we did confirm your theory. There were vertical black stains on his pointer finger and thumb. There is no doubt. It was the Kiss."

"How long do we have?" Mom asked, voice suddenly rising. "Are you sending us out on ships or on horseback? Are we to stay here and hide? Is the dragon coming this hour or later today?"

Carine reached out for Mom's hand and squeezed.

"We still do not know, madam. We have only tales to inform us."

"We don't just have tales," Carine said. "On my street in North Esten…I saw something."

Just then, the Great Hall doors opened. Princes David and Giles stood there. David was disheveled and spacey: hair out of place and sleeves rolled up. His forehead was sweaty and his eyes looked baggy and tired.

"David," she said. "Giles…" She wished she were alone with them. She yearned to tell them how she knew what the king had meant to them, especially to David. She wanted to wrap her arms around them and let them cry. But all that came out was a whisper. "I'm so sorry about your grandfather."

David swallowed, not meeting her eyes. He backed up and gestured for her and Alviar to enter the Great Hall. Mom waited outside, assured by Alviar that he would take her to a safe house after meeting with the princes.

The Great Hall had been cleared. A servant, carrying the red mourning cloth that would probably cover the late king's coffin, exited by the far door. The room usually bustled with servants and soldiers at attention, waiting for the king's commands, but for now, it was an empty room, a mournful retreat from the stir outside.

King Marcel slouched in the throne. As usual, the polished oak chair was in the center of the room, surrounded by potted palm plants, which were also stationed beside ten tall windows on the opposite wall. Despite the ornate ironwork of the window frames and the liveliness of the greenery indoors, the empty room was an unhappy, nervous place.

The new King Marcel rested his cheek on one hand. With the other, he lazily inspected his magnificent crown.

Carine bowed. It was strange to bow to Marcel, but like it or not, he was Navafort's ruler.

King Marcel registered that someone had entered the room, but returned his focus to the metal hoop.

"We have confirmed that the late king had the curse. His advisor is now attending to the body," Giles said as the doors shut behind him. Giles was already all business. Carine knew that he never expected or had a close relationship with his grandfather, but still, she wondered how he felt about it, deep down. "He was a carrier. Of course, no one knew his condition. If word had gotten out, the king would have been executed just as others were executed for their marks."

"I know," Carine said, searching Giles eyes for feeling. Nothing. At least, he shrouded any existent grief in formality.

Alviar turned to Carine. "Shoemaker, you said you saw something important?"

Carine's gloves were sticking to her palms. David looked like he needed to sit down.

"The Kiss isn't random," Carine said, projecting her voice so that maybe the king would listen.

"We know," David said. "The death dragon chooses who he marks. For some reason, he chose grandfather, and Esten with it."

Carine shook her head. "Maybe not. Maybe it's not based on the dragon's whim."

"All we have is guesses," David said.

"No," she insisted. "The mark spreads through touch."

Little by little, Carine explained what she had seen on her street: that one mark could spread to many other people through physical contact.

"That makes sense," Giles said. "We are seeing a rapid increase in cases. Since this morning, three marked folk have been found and taken to the dungeon. One had been badly assaulted…"

"Good thing grandfather wasn't one for hugs," David said, making a slight smile.

"All it would take would be one servant that helped him to stand or steady himself," Giles said. "One touch could infect this whole castle. This just shows that we'll need to check everyone. In the Bastion and otherwise."

"The marked ones don't want to show themselves. They won't come to the castle on their own because they don't want to be put to death," Carine said. "And it's likely that guards trying to arrest them will get the mark themselves. They will try to hide their mark, which will only spread the curse more."

Sir Alviar lifted his chin. "Whatever we do, we must prevent panic."

David shook his head. "But how can we ward off panic once people realize that Uriel has marked Esten for death? Or that it spreads through mere touch?" He closed his eyes and pressed his fingers to his forehead. "We have to repeal the execution law. That's the only way marked folk will come forward."

King Marcel wrinkled his nose. "But wouldn't repealing the law make things more dangerous for us?"

"They already are," David said. "The idea of the law was to prevent the death dragon from coming here at all. Now, apparently, he's here. Grandfather already did the damage."

"What if this isn't a curse?" Carine said. "You must have seen how His Majesty coughed in his final hours. He was weak. What if the Death Dragon's Kiss is just a disease?"

"If it's just a disease, then why would everyone call it a curse? Why are there no survivors?" David said.

Alviar lifted his chin. "There is a chance that it is a disease so deadly, and it spreads so widely, that the tales have reduced it to a curse."

"Well, then. We have to prevent it from spreading," David said, locking eyes with his twin. "We can't uphold the old law that demands execution."

"To reverse the old law requires a meeting of the council. We will need to assemble the advisors," Alviar said.

David scowled. "Either the death dragon is already here or this contagious disease is sweeping Esten. Either way, we don't have time for the councilfolk to meet. Their decisions take weeks! Esten will be dead by then."

"We don't need a council," said Giles, eyeing his older brother. "A king can overturn the law."

"Yes," Alviar said. "That's true, though usually a king would seek council. I am not an official advisor, but only a knight and tutor. For what little it's worth, I'd say that Prince David has a fair point. Timing is everything now. That said...it's a king's decision."

King Marcel forced a smile and pushed himself upright on the throne. He cleared his throat. Slumping forward, he asked, "What's the decision again?"

David exhaled sharply. "Can we repeal the law that condemns all cursed ones to death?"

King Marcel shrugged. "Okay. Just as long as I don't get the curse."

"We know it spreads through touch," Carine said. She made her suggestions to the princes. "Have everyone cover up, whether they're marked or not. Not just extra socks, but everything: turtlenecks, long sleeves, long pants, long skirts, hoods, scarves, gloves…No one should make direct physical contact with anyone else, especially with those who have the mark. At least, this way we might contain the plague."

"And we'll close the gates," declared Giles. "No one in; no one out."

David agreed. "So this is our plan for Esten: Cover up. Keep your distance. This curse or disease—whatever it is—is fatal."

"Okay?" said the king to all present, though it was no more than Carine's group. "Don't let me get the Kiss."

"Don't make contact with anyone and you should be fine. Let's not panic. It's all going to be okay," David said, reaching out to calm his older brother.

But as David stretched his arm toward the throne, his sleeve ran back toward his elbow. As the royal cloth receded, it exposed muscle toned by fencing practice, constellations of light brown freckles, and—at the edge of his sleeve—an ink-black stain.

"David…" Carine said, a lump in her throat. Her head felt light even as her stomach plummeted. "…your arm."

# 10

## ABANDONMENT

David, already weary from King Marcel's unexpected death, examined his arm without understanding. As the realization dawned on him, he didn't lift his gaze, as though his eyes were too heavy to bear looking at the people standing around him.

He disappeared, alone, to his room.

Carine felt cold. According to legend, the death dragon was here, but whether David was targeted by the dragon, or whether he had brushed up against someone with the curse, she didn't know. To be honest, it didn't matter.

If David died, she would lose her best friend. And after losing Didda, she knew she wouldn't be able to bear it.

If there was any good news, it was that the soldiers mobilized quickly: the sick, which over the next two days turned out to be most of the city, were forced to move to North Esten to spare any healthy South Esteners further risk of catching the curse. North Esteners, for the most part, could not afford to rent rooms in the lower part of the city, so they had to do their best to avoid all contact with the ill. Mom, because of Carine's agreement with Alviar, was moved to a safe-house south of the river.

As Giles feared, all the king's advisors and direct servants were found to be infected—all it took was one of them helping the king, and the rest caught it from the others. The servants and advisors, it turned out, had been just as diligent in hiding their condition as the late King Marcel.

There were thorough inspections of the few folk that remained able to serve the new king and princes. Prince David, because of his status, was the only marked one allowed to remain at the Bastion.

The queen escaped the infected city with her suitor, giving brief waves and forced smiles to her sons, none of whom seemed surprised.

"But David's marked with the Kiss," Carine said to the twins afterward, livid. "How can she leave her own son like that? And Marcel just became king and your grandfather just died... How can she ignore that?"

"It's what she does," David said, face long. He shrugged and left the room.

"But—" Carine said.

Giles shook his head. "Don't vex yourself. When we were four years old, she told one of our nannies, right in front of us, that she had never wanted to be a mother without our father in the picture. She spends her time letting suitors woo her instead. She always has. To be honest, I'm surprised she didn't leave the kingdom before now. It was only a matter of time."

After the queen left, King Marcel—under his brothers' and Alviar's counsel—decreed that no one was to leave Esten so the infection wouldn't spread to other parts of the kingdom. The gates were closed to protect the well ones.

Life changed quite drastically in those two days.

Sick and clean wore cloth from head to toe. Carine wore long socks under her long garments, and doubled her resolve to never take off the gloves that she wore to protect herself from contact with Manakor. Going out, all folk covered their heads and ears with headscarves and hoods. Many folk covered their noses and mouths with bandanas, so that their only at-risk skin was around their eyes.

Before long, reports filtered in. Combined with folk tales Carine and Giles dug up in dusty corners of the library, two facts became clear.

One, once marked with the Death Dragon's Kiss, one could expect to live about a week, with worsening health along the way. The mark, which was the first point of transmission, never expanded, but remained in its original form as the body broke down. The disease first evidenced itself in weaker breathing, wheezing, and coughing, subtle symptoms that worsened over time.

Unfortunately, one week was too short a time for anyone to reach the Healing Pools, even with the fastest horses, and of course, any vessel used to bottle the Healing Pool water would dissolve before it came up out of the pool, so none could be brought to the ill.

Two, every patient, without fail, coughed up black tar, just as the late King Marcel had. The tar cough only happened once for each infected person, but after they coughed up the tar, they died within hours.

The city and surrounding areas were bereft of the coveted healing gullon blood, which Carine and David had used to heal Kavariel, despite the vast sums that folk were willing to pay. The blood that no one could locate was the only hope for the marked ones.

All the healers in Esten and surrounding areas were brought to the Bastion to advise and try to cure David and everyone else. Tonics were tried. Salves were created. Libations were made to dragons. Nothing worked.

As all the scholars, students, and experts desperately investigated the curse, their reports came to naught.

The Death Dragon's Kiss…

Cause: unknown.

Cure: unknown.

# 11

## A FIRST WISH

Carine did her best to give David his space, but as the depressing reports came in throughout the next few days, she found she could no longer stand to leave him alone.

It was early morning on the third day after finding out when Carine knocked, and swung open the heavy oak door to David's room.

The curtains were open wide, and bright light flooded in from the windows over the pile of wish objects at David's feet.

He looked up at Carine and grinned. "Is Giles boring you with tales of woe? Good call coming over here to hang out with the fun twin." David's brown eyes sparkled.

She cracked a smile. "You're happier than I expected."

"Nah. I'm not going to die. Why worry about it? Something will come up."

Carine nodded. At least he had optimism, however unfounded it might be.

"What do you think of my new gloves?" David asked, showing off a brown leather pair. "Is this what it feels like to be you? Wearing gloves all the time? It's pretty constricting." He tugged at the tall collar of his turtleneck. His boots were thrown haphazardly by the wall, but he wore socks. He had on long, royal pants and long sleeves.

"You get used to them," Carine said, plopping down on the bed and staring up at the dragon skeleton hanging from the ceiling. She inspected the gloves she wore to honor Didda and to avoid contact with the language Manakor. Her fingers shook as she considered what she was about to do.

Prince David eyed her suspiciously, a smile creeping from the side of his mouth. "What's going on with you?" he said, trying to make eye contact.

Carine saw his attempts in her peripheral vision, but looked instead at the floor, where she noticed a toad hopping over an enchanted quill pen. At least she guessed it was enchanted. "Giles and I found out there's no cure."

"Ha!" Prince David said, getting up off the chair where he'd been sitting and plopping down next to her on the unmade crimson covers. "I don't believe that."

Carine met his gaze suddenly.

David's eyes and expression were soft. "Don't be afraid," he said. "Nothing's impossible." Carine swallowed, but her throat was dry. David's breath smelled sweet somehow, and he sat close, which made her feel warm. "Besides," he added, "if I know you, you didn't come here just to give me bad news. You have an idea."

Carine closed her eyes and smiled. It felt good to be known.

David's hair was sticking up, as usual, and Carine felt the inconvenient urge to pat it down, to smooth his hair behind his ear while he looked on and smiled at her face. But of course, she couldn't. There were many reasons why not, the least of which was the plague.

"I do have an idea," she said, her voice hoarse. "But before I do anything, I need you to know something." She had been thinking about this since she found out he was marked, and was determined to stay firm.

"Tell me."

"My father compelled using his Gift to save me. He became someone that wasn't himself. I can't—no. I *won't* do that. Ever. I won't compel. Not for you. Not for anyone. Do you understand?"

"I couldn't live with myself if you did." His hatred for compulsion was relieving more than anything.

"Good." Carine drew the drawstring bag of wishstones from her pocket. They clattered as she drew the bag onto her lap. She took a labored breath.

"Carine, stop," David said, his brown-gloved hand falling on hers. Of course, their skin did not connect. There was his glove and her glove, and their warmth was layers away. But there was warmth in his eyes. "You haven't touched a Manakor word since that day. You don't have to do this."

"I know." A shiver went up her spine as she pulled out the stone that said, *ilvara,* which meant "health and long life."

This was the same Manakor word that her mom had handed Didda's father on his deathbed. The word had been so fiery and strong that as soon as Granddad—who, Carine now knew, had been Firebrand's apprentice and first heir—took the stone in his hand, his heart failed.

This was the same language that Didda had avoided his whole life, only to become a slave to it in his final weeks. It was the language of the dragon that killed Louise, Carine's sister, and that ultimately destroyed her father.

There were plenty of reasons that Carine hadn't touched Manakor since "that day," as David had called it. Those were the reasons why Carine had thought she'd never use the language again.

However.

David.

He was the boy who welcomed her onto the ship when she fled Esten for her life. He was the one who shared with her the deepest pain of his past and the levity of the present. He asked her often about her Mom and checked in to see how Carine was doing now that her father was gone. He was the one that made her laugh even as she cried, when, about to leave the Bastion one night, she didn't want to go home, knowing how empty it would feel. He was the one that said "knowing you," and was right. He, with his popularity and ability to make everyone feel special, was her torment.

He was sitting here right now, one leg tucked under his body as he watched her carefully with those incredible brown eyes. He was the one wearing gloves because of a little black mark that would end his life—that would ruin everything—if Carine didn't heal him.

And since she had the Gift of Calling, there was a chance she could.

Carine squeezed her eyes shut and took off one of her gloves with her teeth. David withdrew his hand so that he wouldn't accidentally touch her. She flexed her bare fingers, and with her gloved hand, carefully placed the *ilvara* wish-stone in her palm.

She closed her fingers over the word.

For Carine, the pain and power of the Manakor word spurted forth with more intensity than lava from a volcano. It seared, scorched, and blazed destruction within her as it flowed from her fingers to her heart and all around. It didn't just travel through her veins; the pain surged and flexed over her nerves and muscles, and even her thoughts, hopes, and fears. The Manakor persisted in a white-hot existence that begged her to let go.

Beads of sweat trickled over her forehead.

The last time the language had surged through her this way, the drop of gullon blood rose from David's hand into the weakening Kavariel. David and Carine had been holding hands—did she know how lucky she'd been then?—and her father was still breathing, in fact, he was crying for her, spitting for her, compelling for her because he wanted all to be well—had she known how lucky she'd been then? Had she?

Someone, somewhere, so close, had been singing her name, calling her so sweetly and profoundly that she felt her soul stirred like never before. There was beauty like she'd never seen. There was a dragon, her nemesis, being good for her, for everything, bringing safety back to Esten and all of Navafort.

There was something so beautiful, something strong, like Carine had never stood on land, and yet fragile, like she'd never stand there again.

The fire swept through her, cleaning her out, destroying.

Was it healing?

She lifted her gaze to this sweet boy beside her with the hair that she couldn't pat down, with the spot that she needed gone, with the smile that made everyone feel special.

He was leaning forward, saying something she couldn't quite understand, and a cold surge of fear interrupted the heat, slicing even more deeply within her.

What if it failed? What if health and long life for David did not agree with the call of the Etherrealm?

She squeezed her fingers tighter, or tried to, but looking down saw that her knuckles were white and she couldn't squeeze any more. David was still trying to tell her something, but she didn't understand, and his face blurred as something wet impeded her vision.

The wishstone dropped onto the crimson rug.

Normalcy, like a slow wind, restored her veins and bones.

"Carine?" David said, as if he'd said it a million times. His face was wrought with a terrible concern. "Are you okay? What happened?"

Carine steadied herself on the bed, unable to summarize for David "what happened."

"I hope it worked," was all she said, though it came out a raspy whisper. She touched her face and found her cheek to be wet. Her forehead was wet too.

Where he sat on the bed, David pushed back his royal sleeve. His arm had one or two familiar freckles. For a moment, a thrill jolted through her; the freckles were all she saw.

But David rolled his arm over, and the black spot appeared.

He met her eyes and Carine coughed up more tears. Through the blur, she made out the golden lines of *ilvara* as it lay on the floor, and summoned the strength for a second attempt.

David shook his head, and—daringly—pulled her forward, close to him, so her forehead fell onto the soft, cloth-covered part of his chest near his collarbone. "Don't do that again," he said, smoothing her surcoat on her back in long, gentle motions while she shuddered and cried. "Don't do that again for me."

# 12

## STRANGER

Worn out, Carine squeezed her gloved hands together when she left the Bastion through the main castle doors.

Her mind was foggy. Her skin crawled from the memory of the searing pain that had done nothing to help her friend. She had hoped that wishing would work, but now a dreadful realization fell upon her. If she did not compel, David would probably die.

There had to be another way.

At the castle gate, someone interrupted her thoughts.

"Pardon! Pardon!" said a girl Carine had never seen with an accent Carine had never heard.

The foreigner had a rounder face than most Navafortians, and darker skin than anyone in the region. Her eyes were wide, blue-green, and brilliant. She was short, but stood with peppy, confident posture.

The girl met Carine's gaze as though she knew her. "Pardon. Pardon, miss! Please. Excuse me." 'Pardon' was an old word, rarely used; perhaps the girl had studied this language from an outdated guide.

Carine looked behind her. There were four guards at the gate—double the usual number—but they stood expressionless, which told Carine this girl had been here a while, and none of them would answer to the address "miss."

"Do I know you?" Carine said, certain they had never met.

"No, no. I am sorry." She smiled sweetly. "Let me explain. I have been watching you. I have learned you are friends with the princes." She said this as though it qualified as an explanation.

Carine drew in a breath but stopped herself from answering. "Why?"

The girl's smile was dazzling. "Is His Majesty Prince David asking for me?" She leaned forward, hands pressed together. Something golden glittered in her sleeve.

Carine's stomach turned. She was losing David already, and now this. "Do you know him?" Carine asked. Maybe he had met her on some political excursion when he was younger. It wouldn't be impossible. But good Ether, girls should be swooning over Prince—King—Marcel, not his younger, dying, brother. After all, ever since Sophie and the others heard the news about David, they hadn't visited the Bastion.

The girl nodded, eyes bright. "Is he?"

She hadn't answered Carine's question.

"This is a bad time..." Carine trailed off, waiting for the girl to interject with her name. She didn't.

"But I'm—how do you say it in your language? I think the word is 'attracted.' Yes, I'm attracted to him."

Carine laughed tersely. It was one thing to tolerate all of David's female friends. It was another to have to counsel them through their romantic longings. Carine thought of all the times she wanted a moment alone with David, just to find he had plans with his friends to sit at the water's edge or explore the Bastion gardens.

"Well in case you didn't hear, he has the Death Dragon's Kiss, so your attraction may have to be short lived."

"I know," she mourned. "That's why I must know. Is he asking for me?"

"No." The simple answer was surprisingly delicious.

The foreign girl just stood there, forehead creased. "I do not understand. He needs me."

"He needs a cure." Her bluntness with other girls surprised her. Maybe this explained why she had no girl friends.

"I am here for him. Does he know that?"

Carine rolled her eyes and let slip the cruel phrase that came to her mind. "Go ask the Naga."

The girl lifted her chin. To Carine's annoyance, the girl wasn't shaken at all. "I will be in Esten," she said, with an air of confidence that David would surely like. "Tell the prince. Tell him I'm here for him."

Carine nodded, knowing full well that the story of this strange girl would end at this gate. Carine had no intention of ever mentioning or thinking of her again.

However, after a few steps toward South Esten, Carine stopped in her tracks.

That was it. There was something she could do. There was hope beyond evil compulsion.

The girl clapped as Carine ran back through the gates into the Bastion. "Thank you!" the girl cheered. "Thank you, friend! Tell the prince!"

But that wasn't what Carine would do. Energy pulsed through her veins as a smile came to her lips.

Go ask the Naga.

The man-eating snake might have a cure.

# 13

## THE CAVE

The Naga—half-snake, half-man—lived alone in caves. They rarely ventured into the sunlight, feeding instead on critters and folk that wandered in seeking shelter and answers. Their folk gift was knowledge, a knowledge which in this case, could save David's life.

They didn't tell Mom or Alviar about their plans—they would only tell them not to go—but David thought it was a brilliant idea and secured horses from the royal stables. Giles said only legendary folk escaped a Naga cave with their lives, and therefore determined that unless he went, both Carine and David would perish. After a hard half-day ride, the three arrived at the nearest Naga's cave.

David adjusted his armor over his copious layers of cloth. He had been idly chatting the whole ride over, excited about this new dangerous adventure, but behind his smile was the tension of all that hung in the balance if they failed. "If you think about it, this is the last bit of daylight that hundreds of folk ever saw."

With a gloved hand, Carine gave him the slap on the shoulder he deserved. "How can you say that right before we go in there?"

But David's mouth gave way to a brilliant, infectious smile. He locked his eyes on Carine. "We'll be fine."

Carine scowled. David's optimism might help him ignore his disease, but insisting that danger wasn't danger, was not optimism; it was stupidity.

"Statistically," said Giles, dusting off his hands as he reached for their lanterns and handed them out, "that isn't the case. We are fourteen and a half times more likely to die in the cave than to escape with a cure. Most people perish when they go taunt the Naga."

Carine's skin crawled. Even from here she detected a certain stench when the breeze blew toward them. "As much as I hate to say it, this bad idea is our only idea. Only a Naga can tell us where to find a cure in time."

"Well then," David said. "What are we waiting for?"

Carine patted her pocket, double-checking for the bag of wish stones and awl, just in case. Her shield-ribbon tied back her hair.

She lifted her lantern; it was bright outside but would be dark once they walked deep into the cave. The mouth of the cave would be just tall enough to fit them without Giles leaning over. "If it gets too dangerous, we'll retreat. Okay? That's the backup plan. If it gets too bad, we run out of there."

"Deal," David agreed. Giles nodded.

So Carine stepped from the healthy grass into the cool rock.

Naga—she recalled as the stench and darkness engulfed her—never left their caves. They were private folk, if you could call them folk. Like centaurs and fauns, Naga had half-human, half-animal features. Where humans had two legs, the Naga had a long snake tail.

Carine had expected signs of domesticity, something to make this rock formation homey. But there was no comely rug, lantern, or art here. Stalactites hung sharply from the ceiling as their counterpart stalagmites shot up. Together, they resembled rows of shark teeth, and now that David was entering the cave after Giles, bow loaded, they were all inside.

"This way," Carine said, lifting the lantern and leading David and Giles away from the sunlight as they followed the narrowing rock passageway into the cave's depths. Carine's heart pounded.

"Hello?" echoed a young female voice. Carine jumped, just as the girl called again. It sounded like the voice was coming from behind them. "Your majesties?"

"Who is that?" Carine said, her question only loud enough for David and Giles to hear.

Giles unsheathed his sword. "It could be a trick."

"It sounds like a girl," David said, waving his hand for Giles to put the sword back.

Giles didn't. "Naga can be girls."

David ignored him. "Who's there?"

Through the mouth of the cave, it was clear who was calling: the foreign girl who said she was "attracted" to David. She stood by a sleek black horse with a white irregular blaze tied up near the horses from the Bastion. She must have followed them all the way from Esten. Carine wondered if the girl had been waiting outside the gates for them that entire time. And where she had gotten the horse.

"Who is that?" David said, more perplexed than enchanted, thank the flames.

From the distance, Carine and the girl's eyes met.

Her mouth dropped open with glee as her hands lifted. "There you are!"

David caught the recognition. "You two know each other?"

"Not exactly," Carine said, cringing. This was not the time for a love-struck teenager to gallivant after her prince.

"Did you tell her where we were going?" Giles demanded.

"Trust me, I didn't tell her anything. She must have followed us."

"Why?" David said.

"How?" said Giles. "I didn't hear a horse. She would have had to have followed us for hours. I would have noticed."

"It's me! Selena!" Selena. That was her name. She beamed as she sauntered toward the mouth of the cave.

As if echoing Carine's response, the mouth of the cave started to move.

Like jaws, the top and bottom of the cave closed in on each other, tooth-like stalactites crashing into jutting stalagmites. Rock crumbled on rock at impact.

"Take cover!" Giles said, covering his head with his arms and moving in to safety. Carine did the same.

But David stood in awe. "It's not collapsing. It's enchanted."

Outside, Selena catapulted forward. "Wait!"

Enchanted or not, the light faded as the mouth grew too small for a person to fit through it.

"Wait! Wait!" Selena shoved her arm through the hole in the wall, but just as the mouth of the cave threatened to crush it, she slipped it out.

Darkness enshrouded them. Silence took hold as the cave's motion ceased.

Carine took a breath and lifted the lantern. In the new darkness she realized this wasn't just about David's survival. If they didn't find the Naga before the Naga found them, they would perish in this damp, cold dwelling.

"Do not worry! I will find you!" came Selena's muffled voice from outside.

Giles raised his lamp. "What does she want? Why did she come here?"

Carine took a breath and faced the direction that would lead them away from the closed cave mouth and the crazed girl outside. "You wouldn't believe me if I told you."

Her eyes caught David, covered in dust from the collapse of the entrance. He returned her gaze with a warm smile. Carine's heart leapt. As much as Selena's obsession annoyed Carine, she had to admit, she couldn't blame her.

# 14

## GLITTERED WALL

Carine took the gloves off her shaking, sweating hands, and slid along the wall, hunching over as she peered around the curving stone. The twins followed. The silence of the cave—interrupted by echoing drips of water and screeches of bats—was getting to her. They had been following the cave farther and farther for a quarter of an hour. Instead of bringing her closer to their goal, every step and every turn seemed to trap her deeper and deeper underground.

Her boot kicked something that clattered as it skidded across the rock floor.

"Shh!" said Giles, raising his lamp.

The lantern light flickered orange over ivory bones. Not just random bones but recognizable parts: ribs, arms, legs, skulls. Human bones. Faun bones. Folk skulls. Carine's stomach twisted.

Naga ate rabbits and squirrels, but they earned their reputation by the staple of their diet, which was something else entirely.

In the tales, the Naga were called cannibals, though one Naga would never eat another. Instead, they ate other folk types, at least half human like the Naga themselves. They didn't seem to mind the similarities between themselves and their meals.

One would think it would be rather difficult for a Naga to capture legged-folk. The Naga, after all, were hard of hearing and nearly blind. They had small round ears that captured sound but couldn't place it, and purple irises that encircled nearly useless pupils.

However, what the Naga lacked in vision and hearing, they made up for with their keen sense of smell. They smelled hares and birds and other small prey with ease. They also smelled lying hearts—secrets; this was the talent that led so many adventurers to their early demise.

"They're cannibals," David whispered, face distorted with disgust. Carine saw him calculating with despair how many of these dead folk must be Navafortians.

"Watch the statements you make," Giles said, his voice as low as possible without whispering. Even at this level of speech, his voice had poise and elegance. "Anything you say, if it turns out to be a lie, will alert them we're here. Lies have an odor to them the way a hot meal has to us."

"They probably already know we're here," Carine said. "They probably detected us the moment the cave shut." Goosebumps rose on her arms.

Carine, David, and Giles were trespassing in the Naga's home, unwelcome, unready.

They had formed their plan with the only information they had: legends. According to the tales, the Naga would answer your questions and lose their appetite only if you held their hands. It was said they remembered their folkness at that physical touch. The effect was so strong that you could starve a Naga by holding its hands long enough.

To switch off the Naga's hunger was step one. Once one held hands with the snake-man beast, one would ask a question, and the Naga would answer. Their folk gift was knowledge of the realm. They knew things others didn't, but could only access that knowledge when directly asked.

"Careful here," David said as the rock face they stood on grew narrower and taller. They ascended carefully, but the scarcity of light made Carine not want to move at all. She hugged close to the cold, damp wall until something moved behind her.

"What was that?"

Giles raised his lantern. The light fell over a deep ravine that ran beside their footpath, but nothing was behind them. Nothing they could see anyway.

Giles steadied his right hand on the hilt of his sword. "Let's keep going." He raised the lamp.

Not forgetting the disconcerting noises, Carine traced the wall with her shoulder, thinking about the protection stone in her pocket. She hadn't touched Manakor since David's room, and didn't plan to now, but if it was life or death, she could bear the pain of wishing again, and hope that the Etherrealm's will would match her own.

As she led the way around yet another turn, Carine's breath caught. The lantern light illuminated the cave which now resembled a colorful night sky as gems dazzled within the rocks. Stalagmites shot up from the ground like spears and stalactites hung in beautiful, sharp formation like eerie chandeliers.

Between the stray bones and the breathtaking gems, the space was grotesque and enchanting all at once. Water ran down through the channel below them in beautiful rivulets. It caught in pools, which reflected the light, making rays move and dance across the glittering walls.

"Did you know this was here?" David asked, transfixed.

Carine shook her head.

"If others have made it this far," Giles answered, "I doubt they've made it back."

Pain seized Carine's palm on the wall. She shrieked as she ripped her hand away. A familiar bolt of lightning surged through her. She understood the source of the pain even as David asked "What happened?" and Giles lifted his lantern to illuminate the golden graffiti across the wall.

"Are you hurt?" David asked. Carine shook her head, meeting his eyes.

The lantern light flickered over the golden graffiti, and Carine inched back from the wall so she wouldn't touch it again. "Why would someone write Manakor in here?"

"Not only Manakor," said Giles, pointing. Above and below the Manakor words were a dozen other lines of text, all in different languages.

"It's a translation," David said, mouth agape with wonder. "It's the same sentence written over and over in different languages."

"Not just any sentence." Carine said. "It's a question." Three lines below the glittering gold, Carine recognized their own native tongue: *Why are you here?*

To save David. The answer flew to Carine's mind before she had a chance to stop it. She swallowed. "These must be questions people lie about."

"In that case, don't read them," Giles advised. "They were written to confuse us. To make us lie in our hearts, or lie to each other. This whole space is designed to alert them to our presence."

"So it's a trap," Carine said, her voice quieting. She thought about the folk skeletons in the previous chamber and shivered. Carine wondered how many of them had alerted the Naga to their presence because of this very question. "Let's get out of here."

"Let's," Giles agreed. "And let's not touch the Manakor either...if it causes you pain." Giles' cool, intense eyes, grey in the dim light, met Carine's.

She drew back.

Giles was sharp. He must have heard that touching Manakor causes pain to those with the Gift of Calling. Carine's heart pounded so loudly she thought the Naga, even with their small ears, might hear it.

"It doesn't," Carine blurted, to get Giles to turn his intense gaze away.

But even as she spoke, the blood drained from her face.

She hadn't meant to lie. The words had stumbled out.

Carine's face felt cold. She needed to sit down. "It's true," she said, wishing with all her heart that the truth could cover up whatever stink her lie had emitted. "I have the Gift of Calling."

"How?" Giles asked.

Carine checked the stunning, frightening room for a sign of the snake. "I inherited it from my dad. His father was Firebrand's apprentice."

"That's big news."

"I'm sorry I didn't tell you," Carine leaned forward in such a way that it was clear she was apologizing to Giles alone.

Giles turned to his brother. "*You* knew? How did you know?"

"I found out at the Healing Pools," said David. "Let's get moving."

Giles didn't budge. "So you told David. Why not me?"

Carine's voice caught. She was prepared to offer explanations about how blood transferred the Gift of Calling even through birth. She was prepared to defend herself, to swear that she had never compelled—which was true. She was prepared to explain with fervor that she hated her Gift, that it was no help to David, and that it had killed her father when he'd compelled.

But Giles hadn't asked those things.

"This isn't the place to ask questions," David said. "Let's go."

Giles didn't budge. "This is the perfect place to ask questions to which you'd like honest answers."

"I don't know why I didn't tell you," she admitted, beginning to regret that decision. "David's right. We should move."

"I am a friend," Giles said. Carine was surprised to detect hurt in his voice. "I guess...I was ashamed."

"Don't guess!" David said. "Do you remember where we are?"

"Ashamed of power?" Giles asked evenly, an ease returning to his facial expression. His lips hinted at a smile. Carine could never keep track of what Giles might be thinking. At times like these, it was infuriating.

"Not power, exactly." A distance settled between her and the princes. Carine couldn't explain it. She wasn't ashamed of power, but rather of what could so easily become of her. She could so easily turn into her father.

David gave her shoulder a friendly—though awkward—pat. He didn't understand. Besides, his focus was elsewhere as he scanned the shadows for their foe.

Giles, on the other hand, stared straight at her, a frown deepening on his chin. "You have the Gift of Calling. That means you can heal David right now."

Carine swallowed. "I have the power to…"

"Well? What are you waiting for?" Giles' shoulders were square. "Heal him."

"I would have to compel. I won't do that." She clenched her jaw.

Giles' lip curled. Even when angry, his voice was low, slow, and even. "You won't do what you can to save my brother. Instead all three of us are risking our lives in a Naga's den."

"Don't be mad," Carine begged. "You have to understand."

His expression vanished. "I hope you can bear the consequences of this stupidity. I hope all of us can."

# 15

## ANSWERS

"Distress…Fear…The best marinade for a fragrant supper," hissed a female voice from…somewhere.

"Look what you've done," Giles said, teeth on edge.

"Ready your weapon," Carine said, speaking more to herself than to the princes. Giles had a sword, and David had his bow. All she had for defending herself was an awl, wishstones, and an enchanted ribbon. Maybe Giles was right; this was stupidity.

A Manakor question flashed on the wall across from them. Underneath she read its translation: *Is it true what they say about me?*

Carine recoiled, and as though in response, heard a light chuckle.

"Where is she coming from?" David asked, peering into the multiple tunnels that led to this room of death.

"Now you know…what it's like…" answered the Naga, still out of sight. Her voice was distant. Carine wondered if Naga could hear far away despite their limitations.

David armed his bow.

"Prince David?" This was another female voice. A sweeter, younger one: Selena's. Carine's stomach flopped. This was not the time. "Your Majesty?"

Selena must have found another entrance. How had she found them? Did all entrances lead to this one entrapment?

Suddenly, a bright light overtook the dazzling colors of the gems and words in the walls. The beautiful foreign girl with long black hair had an enchanted necklace glowing brilliantly on her neck.

Before Carine could ask questions, David launched around Carine, racing forward to pull the girl to safety.

"Prince David!" she shrieked with relief, eyes wide.

"Keep your voice down," Carine commanded, tone flat, eyes peeled for the snake's motion. "Hug a wall. The Naga found us."

"Do not worry," the girl said, as David took her arm and pulled her over to Carine. "I came to rescue you."

In her hand, Selena carried no weapon. Her small lips showed no hint of jest. She was dead serious.

"We don't need rescuing," Carine asserted. "We came to find the Naga, in fact."

"Did you now?" hissed the Naga, closer than before.

Selena inhaled sharply. With one hand, she reached out for Carine's sleeve; with the other, she reached for something under her cloak. "Is that the Naga?"

But a sudden observation diverted Carine's attention from Giles' answer: at the edge of Selena's sleeve, on the skin of her wrist, were golden, glittering loops. Carine recognized that shade of gold. She recognized the writing. But she had only seen one other person with a Manakor tattoo on his wrist, and Selena and that merman had nothing obvious in common.

"Do not worry, Prince David," Selena said in the accent that made "worry" sound like it ended in five E's. "I am here for you."

To Carine's relief, David looked more confused than touched.

"I knew it must be important for me to come, or I wouldn't have been sent so far. I have never been this far east. This is only my second mission," Selena said.

"Mission?" said Carine.

A trail of pebbles echoed in a nearby chamber.

"It's coming from there," Giles whispered, pointing. "Get ready."

Carine readied one hand over the wishstone, and the other over her hair tie. "Where is your weapon?" Carine asked the foreign girl, feeling scared for her. She didn't like Selena much, but that didn't mean she wanted her to become snake food.

The girl shook her head, perplexed. "I have a whip, but…I thought you understood. Did you give Prince David my message?"

David darted a glance at Carine.

Carine's insides twisted. "Later. But what does that have to do with anything?"

"I told you I am here because of Prince David." She turned to him. "I am—how you say?—attracted to you."

She just came right out and said it.

"That is the word, is it not?" Selena asked. "Is the message clear?"

Giles smirked. "Quite."

"Why did you come here?" hissed the Naga.

Carine swallowed and stepped back into the wall. Giles raised his sword. David put his arm out to block uninvited Selena, whose forehead furrowed as if dissatisfied with the response to her proclamation.

Carine clenched her teeth.

The voice was low, female, soft even, but it hissed the way she imagined a snake would hiss, if snakes could talk. This was the infamous "Naga accent." Since the Naga rarely ventured into the outside world, the language and accent they learned from their parents was often different from that of the local folk. David had pointed out, while he was chatting on the ride over, that this accent was advantageous to the predators—they could distinguish voices of the folk that came seeking answers (potential food) from other Naga.

"Not going to answer?" The voice echoed off the wall. Carine tried to place which of the three entryways into their section of the cave the voice was coming from. "You can't hide. I smell all four of you."

Carine cast a glance at David. His face was blanched as he looked back at her.

"Do not lie. Do not think lies. And don't let the snake touch you." Giles reviewed the instructions as though reading from an informational text. "Otherwise, the Naga will know exactly where you are."

"But...Prince David," Selena said, perplexed, "I don't understand. Haven't you been waiting for me?"

"Uh...I just met you," he said concentrating on the Naga. "This isn't a good time."

"Maybe I said something wrong..." Selena said to herself.

"It's getting closer," Carine said, to get everyone to focus. David met her eyes and nodded. This was no time for distractions.

"Do you have any secrets?" the Naga hissed, sliding somewhere close. Her voice was louder, with sounds like she was smiling, like she knew she would eat well tonight. Carine shivered.

"No," David answered. Loudly, boldly. He turned to the others. "Answer her questions. She can hear the sound but not place it. The echoes confuse her."

"Someone's well read," the Naga answered, sliding into view around a sparkling stalagmite. "It sounds like the few that have escaped me have shared their stories."

Carine's breath caught. The Naga was smooth, sliding on a thick red tail with yellow and white bands. The tail came up to her waist and stretched deep into the distance of the cave, over seven times as long as Carine was tall. The Naga's upper body was covered in a shirt constructed of the old papery skin that snakes discard when they grow.

Her face surprised Carine most of all. She was sickly pale, as one might expect of a person living underground. But she was young too, seeming only four or five years older than Carine, with a dark pixie haircut and a bony face. She slithered over the rocks, not looking or finding her way with her hands. This cave was her home. She knew it well.

Carine tried to glimpse the Naga's irises, which she'd heard were violet, but the light from Selena was not strong enough to illuminate such a detail. Besides, there were more pressing concerns: the sharp teeth revealed when the Naga asked her next question and the glinting knives in each hand.

"What do you want most?" Her questions permeated the air like gas, seeping into the soul.

What did Carine want most? David. Didda. Louise. She wanted the impossible. She wanted everyone who loved her to love her forever. To be there. Always.

Deep down she remembered those days locked up in the dark. Scared to go out, tortured to stay in. With Giles deep in his ambitions and David caught up with all his friends, Carine still felt that way inside sometimes. Like if she told them how much she needed them, it would destroy everything, like Kavariel destroyed Esten. And if she didn't tell them, if she stayed inside, everything beautiful, magical, and wonderful—like the way Festival had been in her child-hood—would go on without her. She would be alone.

"I want to live," David said, answering the Naga's question so she'd stop coming straight at them. It worked. The Naga turned to the opposite wall and slid along it. A ravine was between them.

On their side of the ledge, four early teenagers holding their breaths; on the other side, a magnificent creature, snaking along the wall, blazing past the rocks and the golden Manakor, searching for her next meal.

This ledge was no place to fight.

Giles waved them forward, and they crept into the next passage, leaving the cliff behind and entering a maze-like room of gems.

There was a splash as Giles stepped into a puddle.

Carine winced.

"I can't place a sound," said the Naga, her voice growing louder again, "but I know my cave. You have entered my favorite room."

"What room is that?" David asked, as all four splashed through the water toward another section of the cave.

"It's rare that anyone asks me a question without holding my hands," the Naga said, bemused. "I call it my trick room."

As soon as they crossed the water, what had appeared to be an opening in the cave disappeared into a normal rock face.

"Sometimes it's too easy," the Naga said, wrapping herself into a soft coil.

"Oh Ether," Selena said, voice rising. She pulled out the whip from under her cloak. "Ether."

Carine dropped the wishstone into her pocket. They hadn't come here to defeat the Naga; they'd come for answers. Carine watched the Naga's slender, pale hands at her sides, each one holding a blade. Once Carine held those hands, they'd have the key to David's cure.

"David," Carine said. "Arm your bow, please."

David nodded. He was already pulling the arrow into place.

"Wait!" Selena said, throwing her hands up. "Do not kill her! She is folk, like us! We are in her cave."

"We're not trying to kill her," David said.

"Good," Selena said, falling back with her shoulders down. She took up her whip again, shaking her head as though something was wrong.

At this the Naga, sensing something new in the air, changed her plans. She slithered closer, nearer and nearer to the water that separated them. She closed her blind eyes and listened, lips relaxed with the hint of a serene smile.

"You may as well surrender now. Fighting back is what the others did before becoming skeletons in my entryway." Her blade glinted through the air. Selena shrieked as it hit the stone next to Giles.

The Naga twitched, knowing she'd missed.

Carine's heart pounded.

"Split up," Giles said, directing Selena and David to the right. Carine followed Giles, careful to watch David. She didn't trust this new girl, and for all her assurances that "I am here for you," she seemed not to understand what Carine and the princes were trying to do.

Giles stopped behind a stalagmite. Carine nodded at him and kept going, tracing the edge of the wall.

"Are you afraid to die?" the Naga said in a voice that penetrated the soul.

Carine swallowed, and the thought "Yes! Yes I am!" made her hesitate as her Didda-made shoes stopped in front of the water. The water wasn't terribly wide on this side. If she jumped across, perhaps the Naga wouldn't hear the water; she wouldn't know Carine was coming.

"I'm not," whispered Selena across the cave. She crouched behind David, however, which to Carine, made the girl's answer suspicious. David turned, surprised by her answer. He raised both eyebrows, a sure sign he was duly impressed.

Carine's cheeks flushed. She wished she had answered that way.

"What?" asked Selena when she caught David looking.

"I'm not afraid either," David said, standing straight and re-aiming his bow.

The Naga smiled. Her expression transitioned from serenity to satisfaction. She turned directly to David. "There is a difference between what's true and what one wants to be true."

Instead of throwing the blade, the Naga lunged.

Selena let out a blood-curdling scream. David released the arrow.

The Naga and the arrowhead zoomed toward each other. It hit her right shoulder. She staggered back.

The Naga's blind eyes were wide, and now, closer to Selena's light, Carine could see that they were indeed violet. There was a moment of stunned silence. Then, she moaned. Her pain turned to anger in an instant. The Naga shot forward, baring her teeth, shooting over the water with a splash. Her hands stretched out, in preparation to slit David's throat.

He wasn't ready with another arrow. Not even close.

Selena shrieked again.

"You don't want to do that!" Carine blurted. Loud. Loud enough to be heard over the others' screams. True enough to stop the Naga in her track.

The Naga turned toward Carine as if she could see her.

"You don't want to touch Prince David," Carine repeated. "Trust me."

The Naga cocked her head and changed course, slithering in a circle around the chamber. David and Selena shot right, back toward the entrance. Giles stood his ground with elegance, poised to slice.

The Naga inhaled and touched the open air with her tongue. "You speak the truth...Why? Why shouldn't I devour him right now?"

"He has the Death Dragon's Kiss," Carine stepped closer, watching every flicker of the Naga's hands.

"But you should know that, shouldn't you?" David asked.

The Naga let her tongue out to taste the air. She slithered, thinking, recalculating her approach. "It doesn't work that way. The Naga are wise, but we can only know new things when asked a question ourselves, and even then, we rarely remember what we've learned."

Now. Carine darted to the Naga. Her hands reached for the Naga's hands, but just as her boots splashed into the water, the Naga reacted. Her tail convulsed, whipping around the cave over the stone.

The colored tail was as high as Carine's knees. Before she knew it, the tail looped around her twice. Warm muscles tightened under the soft bright scales. The constricting tail plastered Carine's arms to her body. The Naga looked on. The arrow was still stuck in the creature's shoulder, but she seemed to have accepted the pain.

Carine wanted to plead with her to stop, but no breath came.

Until Giles' sword sliced the muscle. The Naga yowled. For a split second, the tail released its hold.

Carine fell to the ground; she hadn't even noticed that the Naga had lifted her off the floor. The tail ribboned through the air and as it whacked the ground, all Carine's instincts told her to run. If the tail didn't crush her, the Naga would constrict her again.

But this was her only chance.

In the Naga's pain, she had dropped the final blade. Carine leaped up, climbed the moving tail, and the Naga, less surprised now, knew what Carine was doing.

But it was too late. With all the strength Carine could muster, she jumped up for the Naga's hands. She reached one papery hand, then caught the other, and the Naga calmed.

Carine's breathing slowed. The Naga's tail flexed under her feet; she wavered and kept her balance. Up close, if you ignored the tail, the Naga looked…normal. She had small eyebrows and small ears but even still, if she had human or faun legs she could almost pass for an Estener.

The Naga locked her blind eyes on Carine, resignation souring her face. "What do you want to know?"

In the silence that followed, Carine realized that Selena and the princes must have been shouting something while Carine was trying to reach the creature's hands. They went silent now, and as all the different things that Carine wanted to know flashed through her mind, it occurred to her that she could ask anything she wanted.

There were big questions she maybe didn't want answered. Was Didda happy now? Was Carine fated to loneliness as Thabo had said?

And there were the little ones. These tempted her most. If she asked, "How does David feel about me?" he would hear her. Worse, she could end up disappointed.

None of those questions were the reason they came. She glanced back at the middle prince, cloaked head to toe, dying.

"Where is the nearest gullon blood?" Carine asked, turning back to the Naga's violet eyes.

The snake-woman closed her eyes and answered. As the words spilled forth, her eyes shifted back and forth under the thin skin of her eyelids. "There is a drop of gullon blood in a small glass bottle under a stone beside a short palm tree on the southernmost shore of Ilmaria. It is next to a house with blue shutters..."

The Naga continued as David punched a wall below. "No!"

"What is wrong?" Selena asked.

Ilmaria was too far. Travel and hunting down that particular spot would take over two weeks. By then David would be dead.

"All this way for nothing," David said, and grew silent.

Carine interrupted the rest of the Naga's description. "How can we cure David? Can we cure him in time? Will he live?"

The Naga pressed her lips together for a moment. "I cannot know the future. There are limits on my access to knowledge. Only one person in Navafort knows what the Death Dragon's Kiss really is, but the curse protects itself. It blocks my knowledge." Her eyes moved back and forth under her eyelids.

"Who? Who is this person?"

"His name is Heino."

"Who is that?" Carine asked.

"He is a botanist."

"A botanist?" David said.

"They study plants," Giles said, deadpan.

David rolled his eyes. "I know what a botanist is. We have one at the Bastion. He's overseen the Bastion gardens for over ten years."

"Is his name Heino?" Giles asked.

David shook his head. "I can't remember."

"How does Heino the botanist know about the Death Dragon's Kiss?" Carine asked.

"Heino doesn't just care for plants. He looks deeper, observes their responses to the call. He used to work among fauns to tend their gardens. Even his name, Heino, was one he accepted from the fauns." The Naga's eyes moved fast beneath their lids.

"Where does he live?" Carine asked.

The creature answered with a twitch of her lips. "It is a dangerous place."

# 16

## HELD HANDS

Heino's cottage was just where the Naga had said, and it was just as she described it. Gardens spilled from the round house as though the home were a mouth and flowers were its breath. There were tiny, beautiful peach trees, enormous oaks scraping the skies, colorful autumn blooms carpeting the landscape.

They almost hadn't escaped the cave. After the Naga described Heino's location, Carine was about to release the creature's hands, when Giles shouted, "Don't let go! There is one essential question left."

He hadn't supplied the question, but after a moment, Carine understood.

"How do we get out of here safely?" she asked with a sliver of pride. She liked that Giles, who knew the key question, hadn't spoiled it for her, but allowed her to figure it out herself.

The Naga scowled. "Most get their answers and try to leave, only to be trapped and devoured. Since you asked, I must tell you the way out..."

And she did. If she hadn't answered, or if Carine hadn't asked, they would have carried knowledge of Heino's whereabouts to their deaths inside the dark cave, where no red burial would store their bodies, but where vermin would lick their bones clean.

To Carine's relief, Selena had insisted on not joining them (not that she'd been invited). She had mounted her sleek black horse outside the cave with a puzzled expression.

"I think I have done something wrong. I have made a mistake," she had said, more to herself than to anyone else. She held the reins with one hand, rubbing her own tattooed wrist with the other, as though it were wounded. "Something is wrong."

Selena's absence left Carine free to enjoy the mission. It was as before: the three of them on a quest together. No distractions.

"It's breathtaking," Carine said, dismounting the horse in front of the cottage just before dusk. The brown horse whinnied as Carine tied her up to a blossoming tree. She patted the horse, inspired to compassion by the beautiful countryside. This horse had done her a great service; in the months since their return, Carine had learned to ride.

"What I don't understand is why the Naga said this place is dangerous," David said, adjusting his bow on his back. "This village has been here for years. They have annual community dances here. They sing together."

"Looks can deceive," Giles said, checking his blade for imperfections before turning with it toward the house.

Carine frowned. "I should have asked what was dangerous about it." The questions she should have asked were all Carine could think about on the ride over.

"I just hope he has a cure," David said as Giles knocked on the door with the side of his fist.

A pang hit Carine's heart. David's optimism was breaking.

Ever since Giles had mentioned her Gift, Carine couldn't help but feel responsible for David's ill health. She hadn't given him the Death Dragon's Kiss, but with one Manakor word she could fix him. Giles, at least, was right about that.

If Heino didn't have a cure, she would have to let David die or mislead nature the way her father did. She couldn't bear either, so danger or not, Carine needed a cure from this human who lived among fauns.

She pulled her awl from her pocket. The fingers of her other hand were ready at the ribbon in her hair.

Giles announced himself as he knocked. "We are the princes of Navafort."

"And company," David added, flashing a grin to Carine. She nodded, grateful to be acknowledged so playfully by a boy about to learn his fate.

"Open up. We have questions for you. Questions about the Death Dragon's Kiss."

A short man with long white facial hair pushed the door ajar. Even though he was human, he wore "living clothes" like traditional fauns, with flowers growing over his shoulder and circling his middle.

"The Death Dragon's Kiss? That's all you're here about?" he said. "Come quickly inside."

The man's deep green eyes skirted across his yard as Carine and the princes entered. Across the flowery landscape, the nearest cottage was just visible, but nobody was outside. Only the birds cooed peacefully; all else was silent.

The man shut the door as soon as they were inside and pressed his back against it. He pulled a cheap sword from its sheath as he leaned back. "Don't get too comfortable. They'll come any minute…" Heino gave them a quick once-over and added, "…your highnesses." He assessed Carine quizzically, and opened his mouth as if to speak, but stopped himself.

"Who are 'they'?" Giles asked, his long, narrow sword ready for fighting. Still, there was skepticism in his expression, as though he didn't trust that Heino was an ally.

Heino had clear skin and few but deep wrinkles. He turned to the window, and apparently satisfied, sheathed his sword and relaxed. "It surprises me you haven't heard, your majesties. But then again, they are killing faster than word can spread."

"Who?" Giles repeated, with force.

"Oh, it's the same as always," Heino said, keeping his voice steady and casual. Carine wondered if that was a strategy he had to calm himself; he lifted a watering can to tend to his plants as he spoke. The water shook as it left the quivering spout. "How very rude. I am watering my plants but not my guests. Are you thirsty?"

"You are telling us that Navafortians are dying. That is not the same as always," David said, a line of anger in his forehead. He and Giles shared the frustration rising in Carine. Heino wasn't answering directly, and time was scarce.

"Death is a part of life, young prince. You live and you die; it has never been different." Heino stopped watering.

David didn't tear his eyes from the old man's gaze. "Why did you tell me that?" It had sounded as though Heino was speaking directly to David, not using "you" to refer to just anyone, but to the middle prince in particular.

"You asked," said the old man.

Giles came to David's aid. "We asked who is killing Navafortians. Why is it dangerous here? Why are you looking out the window?"

"Fifteen years ago I could have given you the same answer, though the situation is more dire now. If I have paid attention to current events, your own royal father died at the hands of these men." Current events for Heino was history to Carine and the princes.

"My father died in the Border Wars," David whispered, understanding something that didn't yet make sense to Carine.

"Yes," said Heino.

"But the Border Wars are just skirmishes," she said. "They only happen in the mountains. Once or twice a year a few soldiers fight over the border. What does that have to do with us?"

Giles spoke in a low voice. "Padliot must have decided that we are weak now with the plague upon us and King Marcel dead. They took the opportunity to strike. They acted quickly."

"We haven't received word because we've closed Esten off," David said. He turned to Heino. "How many people have died because we didn't know?"

"I cannot say," Heino answered. "But my little home and my little plants are far from the border. They must have taken many villages to get this far. They are trying to create chaos. Trying to get Navafort to surrender as soon as they reach Esten."

"Are they here now?" Giles asked.

Heino nodded. "I awoke to the sounds of folk screams. My plants, with deep roots and wide networks, have reported the rest to me. The Padliotians are very near."

Carine felt as vulnerable as she had when her family was alone in their house, knowing Selius would be back to kill one of them soon. "Why haven't you left already? What are we still doing here?"

"I was called to stay," the old man answered. "Probably for you." At this, he turned over his wrist, where golden Manakor lettering glittered. His wrists were just like Selena's and Thabo's, but now Carine could read the writing: *V-I-A-T.* It wasn't a Manakor word she had studied.

"What is that?" Carine said, unable to keep her question in. "I have seen writing on wrists like this before. What does it mean?"

Heino smiled. "There are others, yes, who learn of the world and destiny this way. You know about dragons, yes? That dragons are mouthpieces of the Etherrealm, that they amplify the call?"

Carine nodded. Alviar had described dragons in such terms, and after her experience in the flames, she understood what it meant more fully than before. But that still didn't explain Selena's wrists. Or Heino's.

His eyes softened as his gaze fell on a powder blue flower blooming on the windowsill. "My plants have it easy...they know their destiny. They follow their calls perfectly. Little—only dark compulsion from dragons or...from others—can divert them from the glorious path intended for their lives.

"I and all other folk, however, are so easily lured by things less than our ultimate needs. This word, *viat,* is the most powerful wish in Manakor. Folk translate it many ways, but at its core, it means, *let it be.* It is submission to the Etherrealm. It is perfect adherence to one's destiny. It is the garden's unheard chorus. When I wish it, I am free. And sometimes, I understand."

"You wish. Do you have the Gift of Calling?" Carine asked.

Heino's eyes widened. "Ahh. Now I understand."

"Understand what?" said David, growing impatient. Above all, they still needed the cure.

Heino shook his head, undisturbed by David's question. "No, I do not have the Gift you have. To be honest, I am grateful for the limitation. But I can still wish. And even though the effects are not as powerful, my wish is still passed to the Etherrealm. It is still considered."

Carine's hands and face went cold. "What are you talking about?" How could he know about the dragon blood that ran through her veins?

"The call is a powerful thing. To obey it is what it means to be alive. To dare to live at risk, to be open to gaining it all and losing it in a blink. The plants understand this. Too often we coil back in fear, not willing to live gloriously. Or, not willing to lose." He paused and turned to Carine. "The numbness resulting from this fear killed your father."

Her voice lowered. "How do you know who I am? What makes you think you know my father?"

There was sadness in his voice. "He misled the plants I cared for."

The blood drained from Carine's face.

"Your scent reminds my plants of a man that wreaked havoc earlier this year…"

Carine's heart pounded.

"…He didn't impose his will for long, but I have heard cries of terrible deeds that vines and trees have been made to do: kill, wound, grow away from the sun. It pains. It destroys."

"Stop," Carine said, a fire of hate stirring within her. She hated that Heino mentioned these things, and she hated that they were true. "Don't talk about my father. You didn't know him."

"My plants did," Heino said.

Carine gritted her teeth. "This isn't why we're here."

Just as she said this, David coughed tightly. His breath squeaked and rasped. This was the first cough of the Death Dragon's Kiss. The disease was progressing.

"Ah," Heino said, pushing off his chair with a creak. He scooped up soil in his hand from the windowsill and placed something inside it. He squeezed the soil in his fist until veins popped up in his loose, old skin. "When you hold on too tight, the thing becomes stagnant, dead. But when you open your palm…" A plant sprouted up from the soil. "…life flourishes."

Carine shook her head, barely able to contain her frustration. "Stop talking about other things. We're here about the Death Dragon's Kiss."

"Very well. I will tell you what I can." Heino walked to the window, stepping in bare feet over leaves that had fallen onto his floor. He eased onto every step the way older people did to avoid aggravating old joints. "This," he said, extending a finger to a velvety black flower blooming on a short black stalk. "Here is your culprit. I noticed this strange flower about two weeks ago. It disturbs the shrubbery nearby and stains any folk it comes in contact with."

"This flower is carrying the Death Dragon's Kiss?" Carine set aside her frustration as best she could and paid attention. She had seen a black flower or two in Esten in the past few weeks, she realized now. A black so deep was strange on a flower, but with everything else going on—first the preparation for the fencing tournament, then King Marcel's death—she hadn't given it a second thought. "King Marcel—or somebody—must have touched that flower, and that started everything."

David pressed his fingers to his temple. "Folk with the Kiss are supposed to stay in North Esten to stop the spreading. But no one knows about the flower. Folk could brush up against one now, unaware…"

"We will tell them," Giles said, hands clasped behind his back.

"Can we destroy the flower?" Carine asked.

Heino thought. "The plants are all connected at the same root. From what I can tell, the plant is rooted deeply, not too far away. The Kiss has been latent, sleeping under the soil in Navafort for decades. Kavariel's annual visit had prevented it from blooming. But since he hasn't come to Navafort at all this year, since he skipped Festival and didn't return, his enchantments could not suppress it. The obvious way to destroy the plant's tendrils would be for Kavariel to return. His magic would kill every part of the plant above ground, and his annual visits would keep the latent root from sprouting again."

"But he's not due back for months," David said. By then, he and all others marked would be dead.

"There may be another way. The root, exposed to the sun, will shrivel up and all its tendrils and blooms will die with it."

"Kill the root; kill the curse," said David.

"Exactly."

"But will it cure those already marked?" Carine said, pleading now. Heino might have spoken about Didda's compulsion, but he also had good information on the Kiss.

Heino lifted his gaze apologetically to Prince David. "The best we can hope for is that it will stop the disease's spread."

"So everyone already marked with the Kiss...?" David asked, eyes fixed on Heino.

Heino bowed his head. He didn't speak the understood ending of the sentence: everyone marked with the Kiss already...will die.

"No," Carine said. "Think, Heino. There has to be something."

"I am sorry," Heino said. "Once the mark has struck, mere folk cannot erase it."

The flowers trembled, shaking back and forth as though jostled by the wind. The rhythm of approaching hooves jolted Carine back to the situation's urgency.

Outside, the horses whinnied. Heino, at the window, glanced out. A pale pallor set over his face. "It's Padliot warriors," he said, as though resigning himself to the fate.

"What do we do?" she said, reaching for the ribbon even as she spoke.

Heino pointed to the back door. "Run, all of you. I'll be fine."

Two heavy feet landed in the leaves outside as someone dismounted. Then a second pair of feet. Then a third.

"Come on," Carine whispered. Heino had said to leave him, and this was not how anyone was supposed to die. "Let's go."

"Not a chance," David replied, arming his bow. Giles unsheathed his sword. "As your princes, defending the citizens is our job."

The old man cast a glance at the plants he loved. They hung in bowls and pots from the ceiling near all the windows. They covered the windowsills and half of the floor. Large, twisting greenery draped the far wall. Heino took a breath. "Very well, but if I fall, I ask you young ones to run. I have lived a full life. Do the same."

The front door kicked in.

# 17

## ORANGE ARMOR

Some of Heino's flowers grew in a pot at the base of the door. When the door kicked in, the flowers shrieked. Carine did too.

The soldier looked like Selius.

Carine's hands went cold, even as she held up the ribbon. He had a red beard and a thick stomach. He was wearing the orange uniform of Padliot soldiers. His sword was out, and two others walked up behind him. It all came flashing back: when Selius first unlocked the door with his compulsion in Luzhiv's name, destroyed their house, set in motion the events that led to Didda's death.

David stood looking strong and brave, the same way Didda had. David had the bowstring pulled back and one eye closed in concentration. A cold premonition twisted her stomach: was this the chain of events that would lead to David being taken from her too?

*Thwack.* The arrow hit the Padliotian's chest.

These were the Border Wars, the wars that killed David and Giles' father before he ever got to meet them. It occurred to Carine that David and Giles were fulfilling what their father had started. These Padliotian soldiers might as well be the same ones who had shot the arrows at the Marcel who was never king.

The first Padliot soldier sank to the floor, clutching his pierced chest.

The second one stepped around him. He spoke no words. Instead, he brandished his sword and swung for the nearest of them, Heino.

Heino covered his face and made a soft, whining sound that stirred his plants to anger. A plant potted on the second soldier's left attacked with its twirling tendrils. Its green vines grabbed his face, making him unable to see.

But the third Padliot soldier crashed his heavy sword into the pot at the plant's root; the plant surrendered and fell away.

"Run!" Heino said.

Carine dashed out the door with the others, making for the horses they had brought. Heino could ride with David or Giles and Carine would ride with the other. The horses whinnied, and as the four humans rounded the house, the two standing Padliot soldiers prepared their second strike.

Carine whipped the ribbon in a quick circle and her arm collapsed under the sudden weight.

As the second soldier lunged with a sword, Carine threw her arm up, shielding the princes with a clang. The soldier's weight pressed back against her, but she leaned her whole body into the shield and stood her ground.

In the same moment, Giles swung forward with the blade, slicing into the orange Padliot uniform of the third soldier. He dropped as Giles drew the blade out.

But the second soldier's stubby fingers appeared on the inside of Carine's shield. He gripped the edge and yanked.

The shield was ripped from her grip and, when thrown, it slid across the leafy ground like a sport disc.

Carine stepped back, unarmed as the second soldier stepped forward. But he wasn't after her; he lunged for Giles, who had slain his fellow soldier.

Metal clashed.

Carine leaped for her shield, and turning back, saw the first soldier, the one with the arrow in him, who reminded her of Selius, sink a sword into the old man Heino.

She fought to keep down vomit.

Her shield up, Carine catapulted forward as the first soldier grabbed David by the collar. David's bow was empty; he must have shot and missed when Carine had turned her back to retrieve her shield.

"You touched my neck," David murmured to the soldier who was poised to slice him through with his sword.

Carine's muscles tightened as she lifted the shield high. She brought its face down on the first soldier. He released his hold of David's collar and fell under the shield's weight.

At that moment, Giles defeated the third soldier.

Only the princes and Carine remained standing.

Carine's shoulders rose and fell with her heavy breaths. Three Padliot soldiers lay at their feet, as did the old man Heino. A breeze rippled through the trees as red and gold autumn leaves danced in flittering circles down. Wind chimes twinkled.

The plants of Heino's home stirred in a sad sort of way. Another breeze came and a hundred blooms broke themselves off their stalks and twirled in the breezy air. As the sun set, the flowers sprinkled his body in a more beautiful arrangement than Carine had ever seen done by hand at a funeral.

Her breath caught.

"They must have really loved him," David said, watching the flowers sway with sympathy.

Carine watched David's amazed expression. His sweaty hair was all over the place. Carine saw the flowers grieving and her resolve strengthened. The sweetest expression of love at a funeral couldn't compare to another breath together.

# 18

## NEW PLAN

Since they weren't returning to the Naga's cave, the brisk ride home took only a few hours. As the sun set and the night grew dark, Carine trembled.

They were exhausted and hungry, and worried within themselves about the fate of Navafort. If soldiers were already this far into the kingdom, it wouldn't be long until Esten felt the effects too. Which meant, for Carine, that Mom was in even more imminent danger. Beyond the threat of catching the infectious, incurable curse, soon Padliotians could seize the city.

Beside her on his horse, David was silent. His face was long and his eyes vacant. Carine understood why. After all they had suffered to find his cure, they finally knew that nothing beyond a miracle would save him. Her heart ached.

Giles was silent too, his expression hard and his eyes focused ahead, but Carine didn't understand why until they brought the tired horses to the stable at the Bastion.

David coughed as he let himself down from the saddle.

"Are you okay?" Carine asked, still on her horse.

David looked up, and Carine felt a pang in her heart. He wasn't okay. He was dying. There was no cure.

Giles scoffed.

"I'll try harder," Carine promised. "Tonight, right after we warn them about the army. I'll keep wishing."

Only a twitch of David's lips revealed that he was trying to smile, but hopelessness overwhelmed him and kept his expression bare.

"I promise."

Prince Giles was already standing on the ground covered with straw when Carine jumped down right beside him, her heart pumping with fear for the ones she loved.

"Fool," Giles spat, as though he had been waiting the whole ride to call her that. Carine's face flushed. His anger and accusation stung.

David looked over from the stall into which he was leading his horse.

"David's cause isn't hopeless," Giles said. "You can heal him now! You know the word."

Carine's stomach turned. Giles was right. She knew the word for health and long life: *ilvara*. Inside, she yearned to speak it aloud, to solve things as simply as Giles proposed.

"That's not the right way," Carine said, her voice pathetic and weak. Even as she said it, she doubted herself. Maybe Giles was right. Maybe healing David was worth compelling just one time. But then again, the only reason Didda compelled was to save his daughter. She felt sick.

Carine looked to David for support or encouragement, but he avoided her gaze, brushing past them both toward the Bastion doors.

"I can't compel," she said, hoping both of them would hear her and understand. Giles just scoffed again and brushed past her the way his brother did. "You understand, don't you? You heard what the plants said about my father. It isn't right. I don't understand it all, but it isn't right."

Neither of them looked at her again, not under the blanket of night, and not inside in the Great Hall, where King Marcel and Alviar already were keeping vigil, Marcel with his cheek on the heel of his hand in the chair. They had already received word from a village person whose town had been invaded; he had rushed all the way here to warn them of an army—a great army of a thousand—with catapults and other weapons intended to bring the city to its knees.

"They're coming for Esten, then," Giles concluded grimly.

David took a big, wheezing breath. Even so, his care for his people restored a blaze of energy to his eyes and stance. "We must fight. We must protect our folk."

King Marcel batted at the air. "I already sent our soldiers. It'll be fine."

But Alviar shook his head. "We sent all the soldiers we had…a hundred or so."

"A hundred? Only?" David said. "They're outnumbered. They'll be slaughtered, as well as our civilians here. Where are the other soldiers? We have more than that."

"Ill, my lord," said Alviar. "They are in North Esten, dying of the curse, too weak to lift a sword."

"Then we must hope our small army can push them back," David said. Then thoughtfully, "Or, maybe, surrender."

"Please be joking," Giles said.

David coughed. "There will be more bloodshed. You know that. We don't have the troops to win this war. I don't know what they will ask of us if we surrender, but at least it won't be thousands more lives."

Giles shook his head. "This illness is making you even weaker, David. We will not surrender."

Carine was torn. She understood why they might need to surrender. If they couldn't defend themselves, it would be better to lose their pride than to lose their lives. Surrendering would save Mom.

But surrender was not in Giles' blood.

They all looked at Marcel, who sat up. "What?"

"You are the king, Your Majesty," said Alviar. "The decision...is yours, and unfortunately there are no official advisors left to guide you."

"What if we surrender?" said Marcel.

At this David coughed. He doubled over his stomach as he did so, and Giles shook his head at Marcel.

"No?" Marcel said, as though he were trying to get the answer right rather than make a kingdom's decision. "We won't surrender?"

"There you have it," said Giles. "This is war."

David gasped for a wheezy breath and caught it, but with a glance to everyone, he exited the room, making for a glass of water.

Carine's heart pounded. David's health was getting worse, even as an army approached to besiege the city.

Alviar turned to Carine as Giles left too, who was saying something about maps and plans.

"Shoemaker," Alviar said. "I made a promise to look after your mother in the face of the Death Dragon's Kiss, and I have held true to that. However, if there is a battle here, there is nothing else I can do for your mother." Carine swallowed as Alviar made official something she had been afraid to suspect. "Her fate is tied to Esten's."

# 19

# WARNING

The front door creaked inward as Carine tiptoed into the South Esten well-house, so as not to disturb Mom. The house's owner, a marked one, was sequestered up in the Grunge. Alviar had found this home empty and, with permission, allowed Mom and Carine to use it until the curse passed. Which perhaps would be until the house fell under siege.

Mom was awake.

The light from the single candle flickered over her face. She sat up in her nightgown, wrapped in the bulky shawl she had crocheted with her mother when she was a girl. Her eyes closed with relief when Carine walked through the door. "Good Ether," she whispered.

"Mom?" Carine said, slipping her bag off her shoulder to the floor. "What are you doing still awake?"

"Thank the flames you're all right," Mom said. Carine noticed her long greying hair collected over her right shoulder. When Mom was worried, she always stroked her hair close to her chest and curled herself into a ball. She had done that...often during Festivals, and again when preparing for Didda's body-less funeral. "I feared the worst."

Carine ran forward to embrace her. "You always do."

Mom let out a dry laugh. "I always had, sure. But now you're getting older, and you spend so much time with those princes…"

*Those princes.* She said it like they were bad news or something.

"I don't know what's happening in your life. We don't talk anymore. I don't even know when to expect you home. You spend so much time at the Bastion…"

Carine hadn't exactly broadcasted that she and the princes would enter a Naga cave. Or a war zone. Mom assumed—and Carine didn't correct her—that Carine had been at the castle all day.

"David and Giles are my friends," she said, frozen where she stood near Mom.

Mom pressed her lips together.

"They are. They're just friends." Carine wanted to sit down.

"He has the Death Dragon's Kiss, Carine," Mom said, as though the curse were a reason to shun or punish him, the way the laws used to require. She didn't specify who "he" was. She didn't need to.

"The death dragon isn't coming, Carine retorted. "That's a myth, an old legend. The mark he has—it's from a plant. It's not a curse; it's a disease."

"You can't know that for sure, and I know he means a lot to you, but…it's dangerous." Mom cocked her head and her eyes went soft, as if that would change Carine's mind. "Carine, you have to accept it. He's contagious. He's *dying.*"

Carine tightened her jaw. She closed her fist.

"I can't imagine...I can't endure imagining any of this transferring to you. Remember what happened to your sister."

"What are you talking about?" The shock of Mom's initial concern had worn off. Carine wasn't frozen anymore. She was in motion, already exhausted with this conversation. It had been too many hours since she had slept and there hadn't been a minute she hadn't worried about David. And now she worried about herself and Mom and everyone else in Esten.

"Dragons," Mom hissed, standing now. She whispered the dragons' names. "Kavariel, Luzhiv, Uriel... This all comes back to them. Stand your ground or they'll swallow you up too."

"Are you crazy? This has nothing to do with—"

"The magic that killed your father came from dragons. The wishstone magic that killed your grandfather came from dragons. The creature that killed your sister was a—"

"Dragon. I get it," Carine said, exasperated. "But what you're talking about is too simple."

"It *is* simple. David has the Death Dragon's Kiss. That means that any step you take near him endangers yourself."

Carine shook her head, feeling a lump in her throat. She wished she could talk with Mom like they used to talk together. She wished she could spill all her emotions, thoughts, and feelings and know that Mom would understand.

Like now, she wished she could bare her heart and tell Mom what Giles said. She wished Mom could tell her for certain that not compelling was doing the right thing, but she didn't trust Mom's judgment of magic.

Carine tried one last time to explain, daring to hope that Mom would understand so she could advise. "It's not like I used to think it was. Granddad's heart was weak, and the wishstone caused him pain. Didda compelled; he misused his power. And Louise...I mean, I thought I told you about Kavariel."

"Yes, you ran into his mouth and thought it was beautiful," Mom said, a scathing note in her voice.

Mom never took that tone. Especially not about this.

"It was beautiful," Carine whispered.

"And losing Louise to it?" Mom's hands were on her hips, her shawl hanging over bent arms. Her chin tucked in and her jaw tensed. Her voice broke. "Was the beast beautiful then?"

Carine stepped back. "No... I mean, I don't know." She raised her arms. "I don't understand it... I don't—"

"Ah!" Mom shrieked and jumped back, pointing to Carine's arm.

A pit formed in Carine's stomach. She froze, not daring to look down at her skin, not daring to see the thing that made Mom clutch her heart and cover her mouth.

She only realized she had squeezed her eyes shut when Mom said, "Oh. Good Ether. Thank the flames."

As Carine's eyes opened, the room was different. Mom was coming toward her, her shawl spread over her arms like wings. Mom's face was relieved, repentant, soft.

"It was the candlelight," Mom whispered, gathering Carine into a hug. "I thought I saw a mark. I thought I saw one." Mom buried her head into Carine's shoulder.

"You scared me," Carine said, finding little strength with which to hug Mom back.

"I know, honey," Mom said. Carine felt a teardrop on her neck, under strands of Mom's hair. "It scared me too. It scared me to death." She was silent for a minute, just breathing her relief, breathing her daughter in. "I can't bear the thought of losing you."

Carine mustered a squeeze for her Mom. Despite all the things Mom said tonight that were out of line, Carine loved her. That was fact. It was permanent. "I don't want you to worry about me."

Mom lifted her head and took Carine's head in her hands. Stroking her daughter's cheeks with her thumbs, she said, "You're growing up. I'm losing you."

Carine couldn't help but feel that it was mutual. No matter how long Mom hugged her, she couldn't ease her pain like she used to, and no matter how long Carine hugged her mother, she couldn't shelter her from the advancing army.

Carine squeezed her mother tight and whispered the cry that she felt in her heart. "I wish I was like everyone else. I wish I didn't have the Gift of Calling."

And for once, Mom agreed. "Me too, my sweet girl. Me too."

But as they both regretted Carine's inheritance from her father, Carine's gaze fell on a beautiful old book she'd borrowed from David's room.

It was her granddad Jon's old journal. He had been tricked into receiving the Gift and had lived his life without ever compelling. Carine wondered what he would tell her now. Had her granddad ever faced a situation such as this one? Had he known the suffering the Gift would cause when it was passed down from father to son to daughter?

As Mom released their hug and kissed her daughter's cheek, Carine's breath caught. Hope flooded her heart. Her granddad had taken notes on Firebrand's experiments with his power. There was a way, she vaguely recalled, to strengthen it.

# 20

# TAVIT

Once Mom was fast asleep, Carine let herself out into the moonlit night, crossed the bridge into North Esten, and crept down the streets to her family home.

Inside, she curled up under the same window that the Heartless One, Selius, had once shattered. The moonlight streamed in as a bright beam.

Taking the princes' valuable book on her knees, Carine flipped through to find the journal entry she vaguely recalled.

The pages were fragile after all these years, but Carine could not resist stroking her fingers over her granddad's teenage writing and Firebrand's detailed drawings of the dragon Luzhiv. Some of the writing was Firebrand's, and other lines were notes on blank pages and in margins added by Jon after the fact.

"*Master is different since yesterday...*" Jon wrote on one of the last pages. Granddad had observed and analyzed the centaur's demise. "*Master doesn't like me writing while he's trying to levitate a frog. He uses the word for 'frog' instead of the more generic 'animal.'*"

Carine leaned over the book as her heart pounded. She'd found it. This was the passage.

*"He says specification concentrates the power. To compare, he showed that using 'frog' brought the creature to three feet high in one second. When he used the word 'animal,' the process took two seconds. That was yesterday. Today, he levitates the poor thing twice as fast in each case.*

*"I fear—and believe—that he may master everything in due course. I have yet to observe his effect on people. He has yet to attempt it... It has yet to occur to him."*

The spine bent as Carine leaned to lay the book open on the floor with one hand.

Her other hand reached for the bag of wishstones. Careful not to touch any of the Manakor—she wasn't ready—Carine inspected the word she had held onto before to cure her friend.

*Ilvara* it read in the looping language of the Etherrealm.

Carine recognized the letters now. Alviar had taught the princes—and her—to read and write it, if only phonetically. She was fifty five words into learning the hundred known words of Manakor. "Ilvara" meant "health and long life."

She placed the stone on the open page of Granddad's book.

"Health and long life" was vague, but the person she couldn't lose to this disease was David.

Specific David.

Digging into a box of old supplies, Carine found a strap of spare leather. With reverence, Carine pulled out her father's leather-working tools and sat down on his old stump.

Alviar had explained at length one afternoon when David and Giles were itching to go out to practice that most names in the common tongue were very similar to their Manakor counterparts. Carine knew from her own experience, and Thabo's revelation, that in her case, this was true. Parents, Alviar had explained, grew to know their children slowly and unconsciously as they grew in the womb. By the time a child was born and named, their true essence, and therefore their Manakor names, was often gifted, whispered into the parents' hearts by the Etherrealm. In this way, her own true name, *Karin*, had become, in her native tongue, Carine.

To discover the true name of another took two parts. The first component was to know, love, and accept the other. Carine considered her friend David. To her best ability, she believed she did know, love, and accept him. She exhaled and closed her eyes.

The second part of discovering another's true name was more technical. The letter that made the *d* sound did not exist in Manakor. The closest sound was *t*. Fortunately, the other consonant and two vowels did exist in the Etherrealm's tongue. *David*, in Manakor, as best Carine could gather, was *Tavit*.

Having concluded thus, Carine took up her awl.

Carefully, she engraved the Manakor loops into the leather strap. Letter by letter, *T-A-V-I-T* came to form. As soon as the word was complete, it "caught," the way all Manakor words did when they were written well enough: The letters flashed a brilliant light, which faded back into glittering gold letters in perfected Manakor cursive.

Carine dropped the awl and breathed as David's Manakor name glittered.

She had beheld hundreds of Manakor words on Esten's brick walls and in the Naga's cave. She had leafed through scrolls and bound volumes that defined and translated the ethereal tongue, but never had she written a word—a Manakor word—on her own. Never had she written a name.

As her bare fingertips grazed David's true name, the fiery power burned like a distant thought or a vague recollection. To write a word so true, to love a friend with such a brilliant destiny...these were gifts beyond her comprehension.

Renewed with strength and joy, Carine punched holes in the leather and bent the strap into a bracelet.

Holding her breath, she pulled the leather tight around her wrist, Manakor facing skin. The language's power surged.

It would be worth it.

No matter how much pain it caused her, David's life was worth it.

# 21

## UNFOUNDED OPTIMISM

Back in South Esten, Carine barely slept. Her blood felt like lava in her veins, and her knuckles whitened over the wishstone. She held the Manakor health wishstone in her fist and had *Tavit* around her wrist, doubling up for extra power. She felt constantly awake, and writhed to ease the pain, but occasionally she found that the stone had fallen from her palm and that the drool of sleep had slipped onto her pillow. In these instances, she snatched the wishstone up again and wished. Whenever she picked up the stone again, the pain was sudden, but not as sharp. She was strengthening her wishing muscle.

When Mom was preparing the hearth for the morning meal, Carine shot out of bed. She threw on her surcoat, wishstone in hand, and didn't bother running a brush through her hair.

Her heart ached, her face felt worn, and bags hung under her eyes. She wasn't fit for public daylight. Nevertheless, she shoved her feet into her boots and ran to the Bastion in the crisp air of an autumn day's first light.

With the suffering she endured and with the sleep she had lost, Carine knew it couldn't have been for nothing.

Manakor power had surged through her, and all night David's health was her wish's refrain.

Sure, since she wished purely, without compulsion, it would only come true if it was also the Etherrealm's will. But the pain had been strong.

Something had to have happened.

Something had to have changed.

Excitement heated her cheeks as she rapped at the middle prince's door. "David! David! Are you up?" She knocked again, dismissing the shock of fear that he wasn't alive to answer. He still had a few days, didn't he? "David, open up."

Silence forced her hand. She pushed the door open and flew into his room.

David was standing by his mirror, wrapped in all the blankets from his bed. His face was ashen, almost as white as the sheet he was wearing. "I said just a minute!" he cried, his voice hoarse and weak. No wonder she hadn't heard him. His look was raw anger, but it devolved into helplessness as he leaned forward and emitted a raspy, sputtering cough.

"Soot and ash, David," she said. But David was still coughing. Her smile evaporated. David wasn't healed; he was worse than ever. "Is the mark still there?" It was a question she shouldn't have bothered asking, and David didn't bother answering it.

"Just..." He raised his hand, finally getting a moment without a cough. His voice softened. "Just give me a minute. I need to get up and...help our people."

Carine took a breath. "I pronounced for you. I wished all night but you're not better."

"Maybe I'm not supposed to live."

"That can't be true," Carine said. "It's not true."

"And even if I do? What then? What about Esten? And Navafort?"

Carine covered her face with her hand. "Have we heard any word about the soldiers that were sent?"

David shook his head. "It won't be good news when we do."

"But we'll fight," Carine said. "We'll defend Esten somehow."

A hint of a smile escaped David's lips.

"What?" Carine said.

The hint turned into a real smile. "You're starting to sound like I used to."

"Used to?" Carine said.

David nodded. "Unfounded optimism."

On her wrist, *Tavit* still burned. Even now her wishing did nothing to heal him. What if he was right, if the Etherrealm's will was not for him to live?

"We can't fight without an army," David said.

Carine nodded, an idea occurring to her. "You're right. But we have one."

"They're dying."

"Yes," said Carine. "Wishing isn't helping you. But maybe it can help them."

David looked up, peace rising in his expression. "But isn't it painful to wish?"

Carine took a breath, aware of the name that was zapping her energy on her wrist. "So what if it is? It's our only hope."

# 22

## MASTER

An hour later, Carine and David were fully vested for their mission.

They wore long cloaks with low hoods and white scarves over their mouths and noses to hide their identities. Besides gloves, socks, and long sleeves, they wrapped white cloth around any bare skin (necks and wrists) so that no transfer of the death dragon's curse would accompany their journey. Neither would David spread the curse to someone else nor would Carine incur the disease herself from a marked one.

Carine gripped a roll of leather in her fist. In her pocket was the awl for recording the sick soldiers' names on the leather. The way Carine saw it, she might manage wishing for a dozen or two dozen soldiers before the pain became too much. It wasn't much, but it could be a start.

David's skin was ashen and sickly, but he braced the autumn chill with that spark in his eyes that made his smile as infectious as the curse. Carine caught his smile and trekked confidently over the bridge into the Grunge.

Giles stayed back, strategizing with Alviar and the king. King Marcel, for his part, had retired to a mid-morning nap in his room. Giles and Alviar planned the next move for the kingdom while Carine held the healing weapon to fight against that inky plant of death.

"There it is," David said, stopping once they'd ventured into North Esten. His contagious smile faded, stripping his expression down to sobriety and illness. He nudged the black petals with the edge of his boot. A puff of black dust showered onto the leather.

It wasn't the only black flower. The species stretched up to the Grunge and out toward the sea.

David stooped low and ripped the flower from the earth. A trail of root ripped up nearby, stretching to the next bloom and the next and the next. David yanked until the rope was several yards long and his face was red with fury.

"It's no use," Carine said, touching his covered shoulder with her gloved hand before he passed out from exertion. "It'll grow right back."

David stopped and stood erect. He panted to catch his breath, but his lungs squeaked and wheezed like never before.

He coughed into his glove, tears catching in his lashes when he squeezed his eyes shut.

Carine's heart ached. "We can avoid the root for now, but we can't avoid Padliot's army. First things first."

He let out a sigh.

"First things first," she repeated, leading him away from the deadly rope of black blooms toward the wailing, crying, and coughing in the north.

And as she did so, a flash of motion caught her eye. Selena, the foreign girl, stood in the shadows of a nearby building, watching them both. She darted back when she saw Carine looking and disappeared.

The marked ones were mostly together. There was a street in the center of North Esten near the Hopping Rabbit, the tavern that Carine used to visit to listen to town news after Festival. Today, inside the tavern and all the buildings were cots. Through the windows, Carine could see the writhing bodies of the ill, suffering in their beds. The healthier ones, also marked with the stain of death, served them water and prepared the food. Outside, in the square, a dozen folk sat around a fire, mostly menfolk, but a few fauns here and there. They told stories in low voices despite coughing. Nobody seemed to have bathed.

It smelled. It smelled like smoke and mire and something else that Carine couldn't name until a weeping man emerged from a building with a sheet-covered body. As he passed, the others went silent, except for some terrible coughs. The ones who were able pressed their fingers to their lips and spread their hands open wide in the funeral gesture.

The man himself coughed hoarsely as he carried the body out of the square, but when others offered to help him, he refused.

Carine couldn't see David's face behind his scarf, but comparing him to the others here, he was not as healthy as she would have guessed. There were others, the worse-off ones, the ones who wouldn't—or couldn't—spend their last hours indoors. They huddled alone against the bases of buildings, sometimes sprawled on the cold and bumpy cobblestones. Their faces were grey, but they weren't coughing anymore. They took little, wheezy breaths and gazed out into nowhere, as though they were waiting miserably for a carriage. Or, rather, for a dragon of death.

She didn't realize she was frozen, staring, until David's gloved hand took hers. His grip was nice, but weaker than before, so much weaker than when they held hands to approach the dragon.

"There," David said, pointing through a bleary window at a man shivering under a blanket inside. He had a streak, more a like a slab, of the mark across his forehead. "That's one. He's a great knight, good with knives. I don't...I don't remember his name." David curled back his finger. "This isn't fair for these people."

Carine nodded, regretfully releasing David's hand to push the door open. "Let's just hope it works," she said, for more reasons than one.

"Who are you?" said the woman tending to the soldier, though she looked no better off than him. She picked up a rolling pin and waved it at them. "Show your faces." It was clear from their clothes that these were South Esten folk. The woman's indigo and white garment must have glittered the week before, but even a few days of continuous wear in these conditions dulled the fabric of its charm.

David shook his head. "We didn't come to reveal ourselves, but neither did we come to frighten you." It never ceased to amaze Carine how royal David sounded when he spoke to his subjects. For a moment, she worried that it would give their identities away. David had insisted—for their own protection—that they didn't reveal themselves. If this idea worked, folk might hunt them down if they knew their identities. Carine had agreed.

"You are a soldier, aren't you?" David asked.

The man sat up in his cot, and Carine noted the glint of a knife sticking out from his fist. "Who's asking?"

"We need your name," said Carine.

With that, the woman sprung from her cot and thwacked Carine across the shoulder with the pin. "You are going to execute him! You are writing his name to get money from the government or something! You are trying to kill him!" The woman's cries gave way to a bout of coughing.

Carine clutched her shoulder—it would surely bruise— and picked up the leather that had fallen from her grasp.

"Not at all," said David, peeling back his sleeve to reveal the mark. The woman and the man sat back.

"Then what are you here for?" the woman said.

"Your name, sir," David repeated.

And this time, he gave it: Leroy.

Taking her pen in her hand, Carine carved the name phonetically in Manakor into the leather.

"What are you doing?" Leroy asked as his Manakor name caught and turned golden. "That's Manakor."

Carine didn't answer. She took off her glove and pressed her fingertips into the word. As boiling heat surged through her, she wished for this soldier the same way she had wished for David.

"Are you okay?" she heard David saying.

"Good Ether," said the woman. Her gaze fixed on Leroy's forehead.

Carine looked up. As the pain pulsed through her, as her fingers pressed into the written word, the thick black smudge on the man's forehead faded and disappeared. The color rushed back to his cheeks.

"I feel…" Leroy said, sitting up and wiping away sweat that had been on his cursed forehead before.

"It's gone," breathed the woman. "It's gone."

Carine released the Manakor and beheld the unmarked face. Leroy's expression broke into a grin, not just a grin but rejoicing. "It's gone! I'm healed!"

Carine's heart filled. The longer she looked, the more she believed it was true. This soldier had been dying, and now was spry as ever. He had been marked, and now he was free.

"You did it," David said, voice ripe with wonder.

"What's this carrying on?" grumbled a younger man at the top of the stairs, one who was once strong. He had the mark on his knuckles. The outline of the black mark turned bony white as he gripped the wooden banister on the way down the steps.

"Renald," said the woman. "He's healed! Leroy is healed! The mark has vanished."

David held up his hands. "Speak of this to no one."

"Or it will come back?" Leroy said, gripping the blanket again.

Leroy's vulnerability to the mystery of their arrival struck Carine. The mysterious nature of the Etherrealm confused her too. Why did some good wishes agree with the Etherrealm's will and others did not?

David didn't deny his assumption, though Carine had to believe the mark wouldn't spontaneously return. "Just…don't talk about this. We are here on a mission."

"What mission?" Leroy said. "To whom do I owe my life?" His gaze—all three of their gazes—landed on Carine.

Blood rushed to her cheeks. She was grateful the hood and scarf hid her face. This wasn't her doing. She knew that.

Leroy stepped off the cot and knelt at Carine's feet. "I owe you my life. I am indebted to you forever. I will be your servant from this day forth."

Leroy's head bowed low. Carine looked to David for help, but this act of pure submission didn't seem to shock him. He was a prince. Kneeling and signs of obedience were common occurrences to him.

Carine's heart moved with pity for this man. She knew that if she could choose who was healed, if she could choose between Leroy and David, Leroy would still be dying in his cot. In fact, if her wishing last night had healed David, she wouldn't be here at all.

"Please," Leroy said. "What is the name of my master?"

It occurred to Carine that it might not be obvious from her clothes that she was female. It might also appear, and probably did, that she was some powerful enchanter, that she was the one who had done everything.

"It wasn't me, trust me," she said, in a voice she hoped continued to conceal her gender.

"Whatever you say," said Leroy, head bowed.

She mustered up the verbiage that David used when speaking to subjects. But for her, the words came out clumsy and slow. "For whatever reason, the Etherrealm has smiled on you. It isn't me you need to thank. As a knight, you have already made an oath of obedience to Navafort. Honor that.

"Report to the Bastion for duty at once. Be careful not to make contact with any infected person or with the black flower you have been warned about. Your mission will be to protect Esten from Padliot, which even as we speak is striking Navafort."

"Right away," said Leroy, head bowed. But he remained kneeling and looked up. "What about my sister?" he said, gesturing to the woman. "And my fellow soldier, Renald?"

Carine didn't have the heart to explain that they had to focus on soldiers only. She didn't have enough strength to heal everyone. "Go."

And with a loving nod to his sister and Renald—the last one he might ever give them—he went.

# 23

## THE ONE THAT HEALS

"Are you sure you have the strength to wish again?" David said in a low voice as Carine carved the last Manakor letter of Renald's name into the leather. "It looked horrible, and I couldn't even see your face."

Carine laughed drily. "I've wished a little longer than that before." If only David knew what she'd gone through for him, what she was still suffering for his sake. Even now the bracelet bound her wrist in constant, dull, and ineffective torment.

As Renald and Leroy's sister looked on with anticipation, Carine removed her glove a second time. She pressed her fingers into the word and accepted the surge of added pain. The fire burned through her, both cleansing and destroying. Her nerves pinched and pressed. Her organs twisted.

Renald watched the spot on his knuckles with fierce expectation.

A minute passed, and another, and another.

"Renald," David said after a moment, as the pain whipped through Carine. "You're Limly's brother, aren't you?"

Renald looked up, a stroke of fondness in his eyes. "Was," he said. "He recently died."

Carine's breath caught. She hadn't heard much of loyal Limly since his death. His brother seemed every way Limly's opposite. Limly had been humble and unsure. Renald carried himself and his bulky muscles with something like pride, even in his illness.

"My brother died on His Majesty Prince—King—Marcel's mission to retrieve the ash dragon Kavariel's flame. But the King has said nothing of the matter. I don't know his last words. I don't know how he died. All I know is what I learned from Sir Alviar. Sir Alviar is a centaur knight, one who trained me."

If Carine could have brought herself to speak, she would have told Renald how brave Limly had been, and how he had died with honor. With a stab, she remembered that Didda had killed Limly. Her own father was the one who compelled the knife.

While Renald asked how they knew Limly and David gave a vague answer, Carine lifted her fingers from the glittering Manakor for a second. The pain faded away.

Was it moral to use this same magic, this same "Gift" of Calling? She looked at David, dying, and Renald and this woman dying too, and returned her skin to Renald's name. Wishing Manakor like this, never letting it pass through her lips, never imposing her own will, only hoping and wishing she might remind the Etherrealm of what was good, wishing for a miracle...this was different. This differed from Didda's use of his power.

It wasn't the power that was bad, but how it was used.

Only, now again, it wasn't working. At least, not like she wanted it to.

The black mark on Renald's knuckles failed to fade, but the pain persisted.

"Are you sure you're doing it right?" Renald asked after several minutes.

The beads of sweat on her forehead, the searing pain within, told her yes, she was wishing correctly. The Manakor was in action. But for whatever reason, Renald wouldn't heal quickly like Leroy.

"Come on," David said. "We need more names."

"I'm sorry," she said, not daring to meet Renald's eyes. "I'll keep trying." She wrapped the leather around her wrist.

Renald led them to several other soldiers. Carine recorded their names and healed two of them instantly.

"Are you the Ember Bearer?" said an old man Carine had often seen among the fishermen. He grabbed her covered wrist after the first soldier stood, rejoicing, and hurried off to the Bastion. The fisherman's olive face was deep with wrinkles and his bright white hair covered his head and chin.

His wife, shriveled as a raisin, clapped the back of her hand across his chest. "Don't say that," she hissed. "You don't want people to know you believe in that stuff...Ember Bearers, dragon magic, the Obedience... If the royals find out, they'll kill you."

"What's it matter?" asked the fisherman to his wife. "I'm dying anyway, and if this is the Ember Bearer, I'd like to know. Are you?" His eyes were brilliant blue.

"What is the Ember Bearer?" Carine asked.

The fisherman's blue eyes became downcast. "The Ember Bearer brings a healing Ember. That must be what you have."

Carine shook her head. "No, I'm sorry. That isn't me."

"There are no Ember Bearers in Navafort. It's unheard of," said the fisherman's wife. "Let it go."

The man cocked his head, undeterred. "Are you sure?" Carine was glad her scarf hid her face as she walked off. "Aren't you the one that heals?"

Another soldier, upon seeing his black mark vanish, leapt up and kissed his sick daughter's cheek. Immediately, the black mark stained his lips, and he was ill again.

Carine tried again, and the mark disappeared.

"Report to the Bastion at once," said David.

The twice-healed man swallowed. "And my daughter?" As if on cue, the daughter, only five, coughed several times.

They were outside now, and the first soldier hadn't left as quietly as Sir Leroy had.

Onlookers were pressing in.

"Soldiers only," David said, casting a worried glance at Carine, who now suffered eight names wrapped on bands of leather around her arm.

But the little girl coughed again, and Carine couldn't help herself. She readied her awl. "What's her name?"

After scratching folk's names into straps and wrapping them around her wrist, Carine ran out of straps. Unwilling to return to the Bastion without more soldiers, she recorded their names on one big swatch of leather instead. There were forty-one names—soldiers and civilians alike—on the leather.

When David coughed, Carine—who, to save her failing strength, had turned the bracelets outward so the Manakor wasn't always touching her skin—brushed his name with her fingers, hopeful again, with no luck.

Carine had touched each of the forty-one names, and a few people had gone away clean of the curse. But with each name she wrote, the rumors and noise grew, and the folk became more aggressive.

"Please," said a familiar girl covered in cloth, just like Carine. She stood among the crowd in full cloak, gloves, and socks. It was Giselle, Carine's across-the-street neighbor, the stringy-haired girl—along with her brother—who had tormented her for years. Her black hair hung long and stringy out of her hood. "Heal us. I'm Giselle, and under that blanket over there is my brother Elias."

"And your name?" Carine asked a faun, ignoring them.

The faun gave his name. Carine's fingers trembled as she recorded it. She felt weak, worn out, like someone had pulled out her bones and there was nothing strong left in her. When she wished for the faun, she grazed his name rather than properly wishing on it. It hurt too much; it was too hard.

"His name is Elias!" Giselle said. "I'm Giselle. Please!"

"And your name?" Carine asked an eight-year-old boy who looked alone. It seemed there was no one left to look after him.

In a cruel but true way, there was some satisfaction in Carine's hidden identity. After years of enduring the mocking and belittling, Carine now had the power to refuse her neighbor, to make her suffer just a little.

"Please," begged Giselle again.

David put his hand on Carine's sleeve, as if to tell her to wait. "Write their names," he said tenderly.

Carine scowled behind her scarf and jerked her arm away. She shouldn't even be healing civilians. They were here to heal soldiers and protect Navafort. Plus, David knew. He knew who these two were. He understood a little portion of what she'd suffered because of the trio's boredom.

Carine had been kneeling on the street for over an hour, taking names, giving her everything for strangers and people who had scorned her in the streets. And now Elias and his sister?

"I'm writing the boy's name," she said. If she had to choose between the orphan boy and her neighbors being healed, the choice was obvious.

"You'll get to the boy," said David, his expression masked. "First, write Elias and Giselle."

Giselle was watching, trying to understand.

Carine took a breath, inhaling all her reluctance and wrote her stupid neighbor's name. She flitted her finger over the names, hoping really not to touch them.

A lump of a person on the street under a blanket rose onto his lanky legs, restored. Elias skipped out of the square.

Of course.

Anyone but David. That's how this magic worked, wasn't it?

Anyone but the one who mattered most.

# 24

## THE LONELY

"But what about me?" said Giselle, awe superseded by perceived injustice. "Why him but not me?"

"It doesn't always work how we want it to," David answered, as Carine took another name. "Take a seat. Stay calm. Everyone gets their chance."

"And my chance?" Sir Renald had been tapping his foot as Carine and David made their rounds and now interrupted the line of marked ones to vent his frustration. "I gave you my name over two hours ago. My name was first."

"Who are you? Why did you heal my brother and not me? If it weren't for me, his name wouldn't even be on that list," said Giselle. "Why do you heal some but not others?"

The question plagued Carine; hers was the same.

If only Carine could explain it.

If only she could understand it.

"If you ask questions, you lose your chance," David said, pushing her back. It was what he'd been saying since the start.

Renald ignored him and shoved past the folk surrounding Carine and David. "Why don't you heal me?"

Carine asked for the next name, doing her best to ignore him, even though her fingers quivered.

"What kind of magic are you using? Is your leather enchanted?" He stooped down and tugged the leather.

"Back away, sir," she said, pulling it back, close to her chest. But Renald did not listen.

Metal sung as David brandished a sword.

The crowd leapt back. Sir Renald and Giselle froze.

"I don't think it's the leather," the South Esten faun said in a low voice, breaking the silence. He had just had his name recorded. "They're Heartless Ones."

Carine denied it, distaste on her tongue from the thought of those that would feed their own hearts to Luzhiv for his power.

"I thought we got rid of you," sneered one of the unhealed. She spat at Carine's shoes.

The old woman whose husband asked about the Ember Bearer defended them from her seat on the ground, "They can't be heartless... The flame is up. Look!"

No one acknowledged her.

"If you will not heal us, then leave," said Renald, pointing away as he coughed. "We don't want your warped magic in Navafort. Our kingdom does just fine without it."

"We're trying..." Carine said, to no avail.

"Wait!" shouted someone. "They haven't gotten my name down yet!" But that someone was ignored.

Sir Renald shook his head. "Choosing who lives and who dies... This is no work of goodwill. Who are you? Padliotians come to destroy us from the inside? Maybe you brought the Death Dragon's curse."

Renald lunged forward. Carine leapt back, but even so he locked his fingers around her clothed forearm. He reached forward to pull the scarf off her face, but not before Prince David's cold blade fell down on his arm.

In pain Renald released his grasp. Carine flew back toward David, clutching the leather. Tripping over themselves, they raced out of the square into the abandoned streets of cursed North Esten.

Wishing had drained Carine, and as David ran ahead, her adrenaline rush wore off. The crowd had followed: to unmask them, to demand healing.

"Hurry," David said, noticing she was dragging.

His hand reached out and caught hers. Carine had left her glove on the street, and her hand was cool and bare. David's left hand was gloved and warm.

For a moment they were gaining ground, but as they turned a corner, David coughed.

He slowed, submitting to the coughing, which was turning into a fit. His lungs made wheezy tunes.

"Come on," Carine said as the crowd inched in. Her encouragements could do nothing against David's illness. "Come on," was more plea than help.

David hadn't sheathed his sword. He leaned against the window of the ribbon shop that Mom loved, overlooking the river. He held out the sword weakly. "Go," he said. "I'll be fine."

"I won't go without you."

Renald reached for David's hood and got another stab in the arm. David pointed the bloody blade at Renald's chest. The crowd stopped, coughing behind him.

David aimed the sword at Renald's chest. The knight looked down, realizing David could end his life. Just one thrust and he would be speared through.

But David didn't take the shot. It wasn't worth it. It wasn't worth it to hide who he was.

Triumphantly, Limly's brother threw back David's hood and pulled down his scarf as the prince succumbed to another fit of coughing.

"It's the prince," the crowd murmured.

Several people knelt.

"Don't kneel," said Sir Renald, resisting the habit himself. "He didn't heal us. He healed others but not us."

"What enchantments is the Bastion hoarding?" Giselle asked.

Someone spat on the prince's clothes.

"You think just because you're the prince, you get a free pass?" said Renald.

"No, I don't," David said. He shoved his sleeve up his arm and showed them his mark. "I'm sick just like you. And if we could heal you, we would. If we could heal me, we would."

The people murmured amongst themselves until someone said, "You're lying!"

Doubt fluttered through the crowd, turning empathy to suspicion. Suspicion turned to vengeance.

Sir Renald coughed onto his blackened knuckles, then, leaning against the shop window with one hand, pulled back his arm and shoved his highness Prince David.

David collapsed, coughing and wheezing as Giselle hesitantly grabbed the prince's sword.

Carine clenched her teeth and pulled the ribbon from her hair. "Stop it, all of you."

They didn't listen.

Her attempts only made things worse.

"Get the other one. The one with the enchanted leather," said Renald. Even as he spoke, Carine whipped the ribbon in a circle in the air. When the shape turned to metal, her strength was ready for it. Carine grasped the edge of the shield and slung it at Sir Renald.

Renald clutched his chest, and for a moment the onslaught stopped.

Suddenly, Giselle sliced the air with David's sword. Carine raised the shield, re-balancing it as she had practiced with the twins and pushed back. The shield face plowed into Giselle until she dropped the royal sword on the cobblestone.

Carine scooped up the hilt, brandishing the blade.

"Let your sick prince leave in peace," she said, doing her best to mask her voice. She was panting. Her arms ached. Behind her, David was coughing, leaning against the window for support. "We don't know why some are healed and some are not. Prince David is just like you. Tend to your loved ones. Take care of yourselves. This isn't over yet."

The crowd stayed back. The folk wheezed as they caught their breaths. Renald held his wounds. Holding his chin up, Renald turned to leave, but one voice in the crowd stopped him in his tracks.

"And you?" said Giselle, unable to see Carine past the white scarf that covered her mouth and nose. "Who are you?"

Carine took a breath. Giselle knew her. A few of these folk had been her family's customers. She couldn't tell them her name.

Carine had every right to say nothing, to leave them with no information. But something held her back. These folk had the same questions for the Etherrealm that she had, even if they didn't know it.

"My name," she admitted, recalling Thabo's translation of the Manakor *Karin*, "is…The Lonely."

# 25

## YOU

Shedding their cloaks once inside the Bastion, David turned to her with the most incredible smile she'd ever seen. The young King Marcel's winning smiles had nothing on David's.

Carine hugged the leather to her chest. There were dozens of names written; Carine's wishes had cured many of them. In addition, David and Carine were both unscathed, safe in the Bastion.

"I mean, you were amazing," David went on, grabbing his hair with his hands. "You healed those soldiers, then those kids! Not to mention you saved *us* back there."

Heat rushed to her cheeks. She wished she hadn't taken off her cloak, so David wouldn't see her blush.

"You…" David took Carine's shoulders in his hands and gazed at her face, still cool from the outdoors. He cocked his head and looked at her differently than ever before.

A bubbly feeling fluttered through her. Carine bit her lip reflexively, but on second thought didn't mean to draw attention to her mouth. The heat from her cheeks was overwhelming the autumn chill, so much that she was starting to sweat.

David was so close to her. Closer than he'd been in days. His nose was just off the tip of hers, just an inch lower and a few millimeters closer and they would touch.

His lips were so close she could hear them. She heard the tiny pop as his large grin faded and was reborn into a soft smile. His eyes, of course, were brilliant—brown irises that shone into hers like suns.

His finger twitched on her shoulder, and Carine thought he might stroke her face.

Or move his lips one inch closer.

Prince David hadn't finished his sentence. He repeated himself, this time addressing her as a full sentence. "You."

Carine couldn't control her eyes. On the one hand, they darted up to meet David's gaze, soaking in all the admiration and…something else…that it conveyed. On the other hand, his look was so potent that if she stayed within his gaze, she might lose touch with the earth.

David's "you" hung in the air, and as it faded into history, Carine realized that her chance to say something in reply was slipping away.

Her heart pounded. She was warm.

"You too," she said, keeping her voice as steady as she could, hardly understanding all she was trying to convey.

David's expression drifted into seriousness.

Carine swallowed and broke eye contact.

Thank the flames, David changed the subject. But his tone lingered in the same seriousness as his expression. "It didn't look easy, Carine, wishing for all those people."

Carine turned and stepped back, hiding her face with her hair as she walked deeper into the Bastion.

He persisted. "I thought after the first one you'd had enough."

"I had to. We needed soldiers to defend Esten," she said, her voice flat. She didn't dare glance at him.

"You didn't just heal soldiers."

"I know. But we need so many more. Even those that were healed today will not compete against Padliot's army." She turned on her heels, realizing now her stupidity. She might be tired and sore from wishing, but better to be tired and sore than dead in a vanquished city.

But David touched her covered shoulder with his glove, stopping her in her tracks.

"Rest," he said. "You need it."

"Rest? Wishing hurts, but there's still an hour of daylight left. We can save more. We can probably have enough soldiers healed by nightfall. We just need to change our disguises and somehow not get caught in the same mess as before…"

David shook his head, and for the first time since her "you too," he made eye contact. His brilliant brown eyes were wide, his expression sincere. "I need rest, even if you don't. I'm…I'm worn out."

As if to illustrate, David raised his fist to his mouth and collapsed into a coughing fit. The coughs were deeper than Carine had ever heard, his lungs like scratchy organs. He knelt on the floor, his cloak splayed across the tile, barely able to catch a breath.

"Are you all right?" Carine said. "David, can you breathe?"

He couldn't answer. He struggled and gasped and broke free. The Death Dragon's Kiss killed its victims in such a short span, Carine realized, that even several hours, like those they had spent together today, could bring a dramatic demise in health.

Carine put her hands around David's sides, helping him to stand.

"Easy now," she said. "Careful. We'll walk slowly. I'll help you to your room."

# 26

## EVELLINE

"This is embarrassing," David said as they got close to his door. He got caught again in a coughing fit. "I should be able to stand at least." His voice was scratchy and weak.

"Rest," Carine said. "Like you said."

"There you are, brother!" King Marcel said, bounding down the hall with vivacity Carine had never seen. He was awake, for one, and two, he was gliding—nearly skipping—past the paintings and busts on the walls over the crimson hallway rug. His winning smile was different from usual. It was alive. It was…genuine.

King Marcel's blonde waves curled up around the golden frame of his crown, but the rest of his outfit wasn't regal. It was outdoor clothing, as though he planned an expedition. He wasn't planning to destroy the root, was he? Surely Marcel wasn't kingly enough to fight in the war.

Prince Giles and Sir Alviar trailed behind him.

Alviar's usually brusque voice sounded desperate and small, like Limly's had sometimes sounded. "Your Majesty, King Marcel, I ask you to rethink this."

David stood up. It must have taken everything to do so but he stood. A hesitant smile formed on his lips. "I've never seen you so happy, Marcel. What's going on?"

"His Majesty has erred in judgment," Alviar said. "We shall have to sit down and talk this over."

But this wasn't King Marcel's answer. He blurted, "They found Evelline!"

David's hesitancy disappeared. His smile broke through. "*Evelline*, Evelline? That girl you've been pining over?"

"Evelline," Marcel said, as though it were the most precious word ever uttered. "I sent soldiers the first day I became king. They scouted her out and found her! She's somewhere west of Padliot."

"That's good news," said David. He clapped Marcel on the shoulder with a gloved hand. "I'm happy for you."

"It's the best feeling in the world," Marcel said. "I thought I'd never see her again."

David smiled. "So, are Giles and I going to have to fight over who gets to stand at your royal wedding? Do you need the Queen's room cleared? You'll need to wait for this war to be over, but we have good news about that. Car—*someone* cured several soldiers. They are preparing to fight for us." To Giles he added, "Remember Limly? His brother is up there…Sir Renald. Not respectful of royalty anymore. But I guess I understand…He's dying like I am."

Giles raised a brow.

"What?" Marcel shook his head. "No, you don't understand. The Queen's room can remain as it is. Evelline isn't coming here. I'm going to her."

"Okay…" David said, probably wondering the same thing as Carine, namely what kind of king would leave now, under such circumstances. "We'll have the wedding when you get back." There was a sad lilt in David's voice. If Marcel went through with this as planned, and if Padliot didn't destroy Esten, David still wouldn't be alive for his brother's wedding.

"I'm not coming back," said Marcel.

Now Alviar's objections made sense. Marcel was abandoning the throne for his precious Evelline.

David's face still bore a smile, but it froze as his mind did the work. "But…you're king."

Marcel took the crown from his head and tapped David with its gleaming gold. "You'll do fine, Davey."

"No, Your Majesty. You have a duty to uphold," Alviar objected as David stepped back.

David waved his hands out in front of him as careful not to touch the crown as Carine had been not to touch the black bloom.

"I can't be king. I can barely,"—*wheeze*—"stand up straight." He reached out and caught his balance on the wall. "Our people are ill, Marcel, and that's just in Esten. At the border, Padliot is burning villages, murdering…"

"Look, you're going to have to take this crown from me. I'm not going to touch your head and get the curse." Marcel held it out like a baton in a relay, not the crown of a kingdom.

"What about our folk? What about the Border Wars?" David said. This was a gut shot. "What about our father?"

But Marcel didn't seem to mind. "I don't remember him. But I do remember Evelline."

Tears welled in David's eyes, and for the first time, Carine understood that he was afraid. "You can't do this. *I* can't do this." It was only now sinking in. David was becoming king. Marcel was really leaving. "Please," David begged Marcel. "Alviar, Giles, do something."

But they couldn't. They stood there, unable to interfere. What would they do, strike the king to make him retain the throne? They were powerless.

Marcel looked at his younger brother softly. "Have you ever been in love, David? When you are, you'll understand."

"No! Marcel, no!" Alviar said, as the king placed the crown at David's feet.

Marcel's words came out clear. "*I renounce. To time's and realm's end I renounce the crown of Navafort, to be succeeded by next blood.*"

The crown, brilliant gold, faded into cold silver before their eyes. The crimson rubies became blue cobalt.

"What have you done?" Alviar asked, but the young Marcel paid him no heed. He pumped his fist and skipped away. The billowing fold of his purple velvet cloak was the last Carine saw of him.

"What…" Carine said, trying to form a sentence. "Can't we stop him?"

Alviar shook his head. "It's too late. He finalized the resignation with the formal words. It is done." The centaur gestured to the silver crown on the floor. "Your Majesty, this crown must go to the true heir."

David swallowed.

"Young Shoemaker," said Alviar, "I am without gloves, and dare not risk the spread of this Death Dragon's Kiss. Will you?"

Carine had dropped one glove in North Esten. But one was enough to do this job.

Carine lifted the crown with both hands, feeling unworthy under its weight and splendor. "Are you sure?" she said, directing the question to Alviar. He nodded, but when she turned to David, he pressed against the wall, partly to secure himself, but mostly, Carine suspected, to avoid coming in contact with his new accessory.

"Should I?" Carine asked David. He didn't answer, except to close his eyes, like he didn't want to see it happen.

Carine pursed her lips, and with the one gloved hand, lifted the heavy crown onto David's dark brown hair. It lay lopsided, but surely enough, as soon as she pulled back her fingers, the crown was restored to its golden splendor. The crimson returned to the jewels.

It looked good on David.

And stepping back, she realized, he was king.

Unsure, but knowing she couldn't remain standing, Carine knelt. Alviar had already fallen in reverence, and Giles bowed his head.

"Your Majesty," said Alviar.

David took in air, his breath raspy and fast. His eyes were wild and scared as he looked at his kneeling friends.

Wheezing, he turned to face the wall, one palm pressing into the wallpaper, the other flat on an oil painting. His head hung low between his arms.

"Your Majesty," said Alviar, rising to his hooves. "You will not be alone."

But David flipped up his palm to them. The sudden, certain move conveyed its meaning clearly: in this precise moment, to be alone was exactly what David wanted.

# 27

## FOOTSTEPS

Carine paced outside David's door, chewing her fingernail. As evening grew to night, she retreated to the library, near the stained glass windows that overlooked Bastion Park. She liked to come here when she was alone in the castle. The place made her feel comforted despite David's troubles, the approaching army, and what she was about to do.

Carine found a private space. When she sat on the floor under the window, no one could see her if they opened the library doors. Clamor at the news of Marcel's departure had spread throughout the Bastion, but now the hall was silent.

Moonlight streamed through the multicolored glass. A lantern flickered on the table.

Carine unrolled the large piece of leather on the floor. Soldiers' names, and names of others, glittered gold. She braced herself and brushed her fingers over them. A breeze of heat sparked through her, making her shiver.

She had touched one name at a time, which had done some good. But the Padliotian army was approaching, and Esten needed strength.

Drawing the awl from her pocket, Carine punched a line of holes down each side of the leather. Pulling the drawstring from her bag, she threaded it through the holes.

Carine checked the door to make sure no one was coming. Then, working the piece of leather under her undergown, she lifted the leather corset up to her abdomen, Manakor-side in.

The names hit her bare skin like a belly-flop. Wincing, she reached back and tightened the tie. A cry escaped her as the words seared. She leaned over her knees and clamped both hands to her mouth. Tears welled in her eyes.

The extraordinary pain emboldened Carine. She pressed her fingers on David's name, *Tavit,* on her bracelet. The pain intensified.

Carine thought of her father though she didn't know why. She thought of the life she used to have with Didda and Mom. She remembered the way David had looked at her today, and the way it felt when she, David, and Giles travelled back to Esten together, triumphant with the dragon's flame.

And she wished.

That if nothing before had been enough, that this would be.

In the hallway were slow footsteps. Carine clamped her hand tighter over her mouth. She didn't want anyone to see her like this.

But outside, as he moved, the person coughed. David?

Dying and struggling as the sudden king, David must need a friend. Carine tried to call out, to tell him she was there, but couldn't gain the strength to speak. Mustering her strength, she pushed herself up off the floor. As soon as she straightened her legs, a surge of fiery rage flowed through her. Her head felt light.

Carine stooped low, focused, and pushed herself up again.

It took all her strength to stay up.

Clenching her teeth to prevent an outcry, Carine forced her way to the door, just as the coughing person passed the library.

She swung the doors open. "Dav—" she started, but the man turned around. Sir Renald was tall, ill, and barely able to stand as well. The black marks on his knuckles were still there. The blood drained from Carine's face: poking out from his fist was a knife. "Renald? What are you doing in here?"

Limly's weak brother looked her over. Not even his illness could mask the derision at her North Esten clothes. Her expression, too, must have been grotesque, as even now she internally writhed. "I'm sorry," he said finally. "Do I know you?"

Carine grimaced. He didn't recognize her because of her scarf, but at this very moment, Renald's name was on the makeshift corset that was draining her strength. "No," she said. "I've just…heard of you. I…saw you compete in the fencing competitions."

"We are not on a first name basis, then," Renald said, coughing sternly into his fist.

Carine bowed her head, hating him easily. "*Sir* Renald. My apologies."

To her relief, he didn't question her presence in the Bastion. He didn't bother her further, but instead, turned the corner at the end of the hall.

He walked toward the stairs that led to the room of the new king who had failed to heal him.

## 28

# THE DOOR

Carine's heart pounded. As her breath became heavier, the Manakor names burned sharper on her chest and back. She felt constricted, barely able to breathe, but pressing her hand to her heart, she forced herself into the hall and turned the opposite way as Sir Renald.

Unlike the knight, Carine knew the castle well. She knew another set of stairs that could get her to David's room faster.

Carine willed her legs to fly, but the shooting Manakor pain held her back.

She gritted her teeth and hustled past wall paintings and over royal carpets. At the stairs, she wound her way up, clutching the cold stone wall for support.

When the hallway appeared, Sir Renald was already standing at a door, looking at the knife in his hands.

"Stop!" Carine said as Renald's hand touched the doorknob. "You're not allowed in there!" She chased each breath, still standing on the top step.

Sir Renald cast her a look, and for a second it looked like he would stop. Instead, however, he opened the door, went inside, and shut the door behind him.

Carine ran forward, running into the door with the full weight of her body. It was locked from inside. "No! David, look out!" Even as she shouted and hot tears sprang from her eyes—partially from pain, partially from fear—she realized something odd: this wasn't the new king David's door. It was Giles'.

Perhaps Renald had gotten the two doors confused. Or...Carine realized now, maybe Renald wasn't after David. All the North Esteners knew David had the curse and that he would die within days. They also knew he wasn't the one that had recorded the names. They knew someone with him had had the magical power.

Carine swallowed. Renald wasn't out to kill David; he wanted to kill Carine. He wanted revenge for being left uncured.

Except he had made one mistake: he assumed that David's companion was his brother Giles. After all, who could doubt that intelligent, ambitious Giles would have powers over nature? Carine could understand drawing such conclusions.

But Carine would not let Giles take the fall for her.

"Giles," she said, her voice hoarse and angry. She beat the door with both fists, wailing at the top of her lungs. She jiggled the handle again and pounded her sore arm against the door. "Giles! Look out! Wake *up*, Giles! Giles!"

But just as she realized that she needed to warn someone else—someone who might have a key—a heavy metal torch holder ripped itself from the wall and hurtled toward her head.

Carine was sprawled across the floor and unconscious before she could feel the pain.

# 29

## NO MATTER WHAT

"Carine," said a low familiar voice. A quick shake of her sore arm pulled her groggily from unwanted slumber. Wakefulness returned, as did its sensations: the sharp cold of the stone hallway floor, the pounding ache of a fresh wound in her head, and the all-over draining fire of her wishing.

She could tell time had passed: there were the first hints of morning light coming through the window, and the pain of wishing had changed. She had adapted to the pain of Manakor the way one adapts to the discomfort of boots that don't fit right. The pain was duller now, more manageable. Carine hoped this adaptation strengthened her and made her wishes more likely to be fulfilled.

"Giles?" Carine said, registering her waker. Giles' hair was swept back nicely. His skin was tight and clean, and his indigo cape fell behind the silver plates that made him look dressed for war. Most impressively, he was alive.

Carine's heart soared with relief. She wrapped her arms around his beautiful neck and hugged him close. "You're alive," she breathed. "Giles, I'm so happy. I was scared…"

Prince Giles patted her back and eased himself out of the embrace. Carine smiled. She didn't care that Giles wasn't big on hugs. He was here, and that's what mattered.

"What are you doing in our hallway asleep?" he asked, quite reasonably.

"There was Renald…he had a knife…" Carine explained. As the story rattled out, she felt the bump on her head from the torch's impact. "The torch holder flew off the wall and hit my head. It must have knocked me out."

"That torch holder?" Giles asked, pointing to a perfectly positioned torch holder on the wall. The torch it bore burned just as it should. It looked like it had never moved.

"Yes…" she said, a sinking feeling settling into her stomach.

"It doesn't look like it moved," Giles said.

Carine stood and inspected the torch. There was no sign the flame had ever gone out. "I promise you…the flame went out."

"And you think this was Sir Renald's doing?"

"Didn't you see him? He came into your room," Carine said.

"I was in my room all night, Carine. No one came in. But I have seen Renald. You're speaking of Limly's brother, yes?"

"Yes. Where did you see him? If he wasn't after you, David might be in danger."

"David's already in danger. I could barely stand his coughing last night. I'm surprised it didn't wake you up. Renald, to answer that question, is downstairs with several other soldiers that seem to have been magically healed during the night." He raised an eyebrow. "I wonder if you have anything to do with that?"

Her response was a confused smile. She had indeed wished for Renald and other soldiers and non-soldiers all night long, but this wasn't adding up. She had seen Renald in this hallway, entering Giles' room with a knife. And that torch holder had flown off the wall and hit her head.

"We've heard many marked ones have been running over the bridges into South Esten naked to prove they have been cured. Meanwhile, Alviar has been up all hours reviewing battle stations. Padliot plans to strike today."

"I don't understand," Carine said.

Giles wasn't impressed. "To be frank, I don't have the time to review your strange dream this morning. We're at war."

"It wasn't a dream," Carine insisted. David would understand, if Renald hadn't gotten to him already. "Where is he?"

"Who?" said Giles sourly. "His Majesty the King?"

"It sounds weird calling David that," Carine said, suspecting that this bothered him. "I can't believe Marcel abdicated." Giles said nothing, confirming her suspicion. She chose her words slowly. "Giles, I know this is hard for you."

"Why should it bother me?" he snapped. His face was hard and intense. "Why should I be the least concerned that an impulsive, mediocre teenager whose interests include flirtation and desperate attention-seeking should become the leader of a kingdom that—if not for eight minutes—would be mine?"

She put her hand on his arm. "He'll learn, Giles. And he has you to help him."

His eyes threw daggers at the floor. This was the most Carine had ever seen of Giles' jealousy.

"I know, David knows, everyone knows how intelligent you are. You're strategic, ambitious, and skilled. The title doesn't diminish that." Giles watched her intensely. She stumbled under his gaze and went on. "And if..." Carine could hardly say it. "If the worst happens..." —there, she got it out—"...you would be a formidable king for Navafort."

She forced a slight smile as he considered her words. Carine stroked the Manakor *Tavit* on her wrist; a wave of wishful heat flowed through her. "But here's wishing that King David recovers and that you will help him carry out his duty. In that case, just know I will always be impressed with you. We'll all three be together and care about each other, just like now."

Giles looked off into the hall, his gazing drifting beyond the wall paintings and flower vases to the window where morning was breaking.

Carine wished that he would look at her and smile, to show that he believed her, even if it were in a restrained, Giles sort of way.

"Everything is changing. You know that." Giles stepped close to the window and looked out.

"Right," she said.

"No matter what happens," Giles pivoted to face her, and paused, letting that first part sink in. "I want you at my side."

"You and David are my closest friends. Of course I'll be at your side." Carine's heart wrenched as she realized he might mean David's funeral. "I'll be at your side," she promised again.

"Good."

But his answer was too accepting, too swift. She wanted—no, needed—Giles to understand what their friendship meant.

Carine approached, looking out at Bastion Park where Esteners were gathering. They must have heard the news about Marcel and the approaching army.

Carine turned to Giles and his tensed, angled jaw. "My family is down to just me and my mom, and she doesn't understand me like she used to. But you, me, and David, when we're together healing dragons, getting flames, and battling the Naga...even when we're just eating together...it's the main thing that makes me happy. Please, don't let this coronation drive a wedge between us."

He stared ahead, focused and intense.

"Giles..." Carine reached for his hand. By accident, the bracelet on her wrist grazed his skin.

Giles let out a cry—as if burned.

He swatted her away and shot her the most menacing glance she'd ever seen.

"Excuse me," he said, rubbing his arm and exiting.

"Wait, Giles...what hap—" But before she could finish her question, she saw the Manakor on her bracelet and understood: The language of the dragons had burned him, which could only mean one thing.

# 30

## THREE DAY KING

Carine stepped down the hall to David's door and took a breath. The new king had wanted to be alone, but this was information he needed: Giles had the Gift of Calling, and Carine had the uneasy suspicion he had something to do with Renald and the metal that had flown at her skull.

She closed her eyes at his door and knocked. For a moment it occurred to her she didn't know how to address him. "Your Majesty?" she tried, taking the safe route. When no one answered she used familiarity. "David?"

The door swung open with lively vigor. King David stood there at the door, happy to see her.

He was spectacular. David's face and hair were bright and clean. His clothes were magnificent: embroidered fabric made him look older and highlighted his strength. Behind him flowed a crimson velvet cape fastened with two huge war broaches.

"Good morning," he sang.

Carine's breath caught. She glanced at the name on her wrist and dared to hope.

Before she could ask questions, he sailed from his room and skipped down the stairs. Carine bounded after him.

"Your Majesty," she said, testing David's reaction. He didn't object, but judging by his bemused expression, didn't find the address altogether necessary either. "You look fantastic. Are you…are you healed?"

"Ha!" he laughed as they left the staircase, zipping to the Great Hall. He met her eyes with nostalgia as he grasped the handles of both doors. "No, Carine, I'm dying. But if it is my destiny to be king for three days, I'll be the best three-day king Navafort has ever seen."

Carine's expression grew soft as admiration flowered within. David might not have Giles' pure intelligence or boundless ambition, but he had courage and a fierce love for his people.

"So…you're not better."

"I am better, but not like you mean." He rolled up his sleeve to reveal that black mark, that horrid stain that Carine just wanted gone.

Sadness rolled into fiery frustration as she touched the word on her wrist one more time. Why? Why not heal splendorous David?

"…The sun is shining. We have men brave enough to defend our city. I am breathing. For what it's worth, this morning I am breathing. My heart beats!"

He was alive. Moreover, his eyes were alight like he *knew* he was alive. It was a frightening intensity: the attitude that was either courage or lunacy, a way to be alive that Carine craved, a stirring she felt sometimes when confronting the pain of selfless pronunciation.

With that, he coughed violently into his sleeve, composed himself, and threw the Great Hall doors open with a flourish.

The Great Hall never had much furniture, except for the king's throne which now belonged to David. There were several tall and narrow windows evenly spaced across the far wall through which morning sunlight streamed onto the white marble floor.

A few dozen soldiers dressed for battle stood along the opposite wall. There were hints they had been dozing, eating, and chatting, but now they stood at full attention, helmets under their right arms.

They must have been told who David was now.

Lingering beside the throne like a vulture stood Prince Giles, accompanied by Sir Renald. Carine couldn't swallow her disgust. A little closer, watching proudly as David stood in the doorway, was their tutor, Sir Alviar. He looked tired but pleased, and led the soldiers in the bow they took in unison.

With that, the Honorable Majesty, successor to all the Marcels, King David of Navafort, strode to the throne—*his* throne—in four large steps, gathered up his cape, and sat.

Carine's forehead sweat. David had to know about Giles. She wondered how long Giles had had his powers, and if he had taken the Gift of Calling from her somehow, or worse, if he had taken it from Didda. It crossed her mind all the ways the Giles had lied and manipulated her: had he had the Gift when he first found out about hers? Had he had the power to heal David all along and guilted Carine anyway? Had he been studying Manakor in lessons with them just to bolster his own power?

If this was the case, how could Giles ask her to stay at his side? He lied. He continued to lie.

He, probably, was the one who commanded the fixture to hit her last night, and tried to make her doubt herself. Whatever his motives, they weren't pure, and as David opened his mouth to speak, Carine had the dark sensation that the implications of Giles' deception were only beginning to unfold.

"Prepare for battle!" King David decreed in the largest voice he could muster. The stone floors and the dedicated attention of healed Sir Leroy and the other soldiers made every word crystal clear. But David's decree had caused a flare in his illness. He coughed as subtly as possible and pasted on a new smile for his subjects.

"Prepare for battle," King David repeated, his voice coming back. "First, defend Esten. Then, push the Padliotians out of our land and destroy the root of this plague. Messengers," David eyed two centaurs in the corner. "Send an envoy to Padliot's king. He will not take advantage of us any longer. It's time to end these Border Wars."

A chill crawled over Carine's skin. The Border Wars had killed David and Giles' father. Carine understood the desire to crush the enemy that killed a loved one; she had felt the same hatred for Kavariel for killing Louise. But final defeat of Padliot would not be easy. It would cost many lives.

The victory was one Navafort hungered for.

David paused, eyes settling on his soldiers. "It is time to end this. But not blindly. Not without discourse. Tell the Padliotian king he and I need to talk.

"I wrote a letter last night," he said, producing it from the folds of his majestic attire. "Give it to him."

He gestured for one of the centaur messengers to come forward. It was kingly, the way he made the people come to him, and to be honest it struck Carine as not quite the David she knew. But she realized as the centaur took the scroll, bowed, and returned to the ranks, that David sat—slumped, more like—because after all the activity of getting here, he now lacked the strength to stand.

"You think a conversation will make Padliot stand down?" said a loud, clear voice. Everyone turned as Prince Giles clicked over the marble floors toward the throne. His hands were clasped and his jaw high up. He cast Carine a snide smile that made her uncomfortable.

Carine's heart pounded. This was David's first day as king. If Giles had to challenge David, the least he could do was to challenge him in private.

"I have made my decision," David said, though his voice wavered. He coughed a few times into his sleeve, and when he looked back up, his skin was as thin as ever.

"It's a bit weak, isn't it?" Giles breathed as though it were an aside. But everything spoken in this pin-drop quiet chamber was public. "After all Padliot has done to our people in the kingdom's fringes, now is the time to annihilate them. Don't just drive them back; take Padliot for ourselves."

Giles didn't carry passion in his voice. He hardly ever did. But he stated that last sentence with all the certainty of fact.

"Let's consult in private, Giles," David said, eyes darting from Giles to Carine to Alviar to all the soldiers. He waved his hand toward the soldiers. "Um...you can go now."

Alviar stepped up, announcing David's message in more regal terms. "You are dismissed."

"Dismissed..." David repeated. His head must have been swimming. "That's what I meant."

The soldiers muttered among themselves, when all of a sudden, Giles spoke again, projecting his voice as though in a stage play.

"I'm afraid a petition will be rather ineffective...my king."

David had been hoisting himself up with the arms of the throne. The way Giles said "my king" made him stop trying. He sank back into the chair and cocked his head.

"Don't mock," David said, pulling out a part smile he used when he wanted to believe the best in someone. His eyebrows knit as he tracked his twin. "Giles, what are you playing at?"

The murmur and noise of the dismissed soldiers had ceased; everyone froze to watch the new king respond to a challenger.

A knot tugged at Carine's stomach. David and Giles were brothers. This shouldn't be happening.

"I simply mean to say that Padliot is unlikely to believe your peaceful intentions when we already have an army attacking them at their western border." Giles' face had not one crease of concern. His thin lips were straight across his face. His brows were raised with the smug contempt of one who had laid his plans carefully.

"I never sanctioned that," said King David, a tremor in his voice.

The soldiers were whispering.

"*You* wouldn't have," said Giles. "You have been king all of ten hours. It was your predecessor who gave the order."

"You will remember your place, young prince," warned Sir Alviar.

But David put up his hand and leaned forward to hear Giles out. "Marcel? But why? When has Marcel done anything?"

"We've been tolerating these Border skirmishes long enough, David, and you know it. Their invasion is an insult—and worse."

Sir Alviar lifted his chin, knuckles whitening as he respected David's direction to stay back.

Carine's heart pounded double-time. Giles' message wasn't passed along from his older brother. Giles had planned it. He had convinced Marcel somehow. He must have orchestrated the attack on the western front even as David and Carine had been scouring North Esten for any available soldier to destroy the root.

"This was your idea," David panted from his chair.

"You'll thank me later. And if you want to be any good as king, you'll heed my counsel too."

"Who do you think you are, Giles?" David spat. "You would never have spoken to grandfather this way." His arm flew out to all the bystanders. "And in front of subjects? What gives you the right...?"

In the most Giles way, he lifted an eyebrow. "A mere eight-minute flub on nature's part. How did you describe it, Carine?" Carine froze, sweat building up on her hairline. "You said I'm more intelligent, strategic, skilled; I'd be a formidable king... Did I leave anything out?"

"That's not what I meant." The raw pain of betrayal crossed David's face as she spoke. "David... that isn't what I meant."

"*King* David!" he said, raising his arms in frustration. Carine shivered at the suddenness and fairness of his outburst. She should have recognized that this was not the situation in which to address him informally. If Giles refused to support his title, she at least could. "King! I'm a king!"

The bystanders stepped back.

"Can't I do this one good thing before I go? Can't I leave one small legacy? Please?" His gaze melted toward his brother. "Come on. What are you trying to do to me? It'll be three days or less. Do whatever you want when I die."

Carine shook her head. He couldn't be thinking like that. He couldn't be thinking this was some kind of countdown. She would stop the curse from killing him. She'd find a way.

"Giles twisted my words...Your Majesty." She had to tell him she hadn't betrayed him. He had to know. But she wouldn't disrespect his position again. Not now.

His Majesty King David leaned back, knuckles rubbing his sweating brow.

"It wasn't like that," she protested, but David wheezed in the throne, staring up at the ceiling through wet eyelashes.

"I believe you," he mumbled, not looking down. Carine sighed relief, though now she felt the burden he must be bearing.

"Tell me truly, David," Giles said, stepping forward. He completely ignored his brother's request for proper title usage. "Do you really believe a failing student should be king?"

David gripped the end of the chair again, knuckles white as bone. He turned to Alviar. "Why didn't you stop him? Why didn't you tell me?"

Alviar bowed low. "King Marcel was convinced, and as the king's soldier I had to respect his decision. I had no idea that your brother would ever abdicate. I believed the last Marcel would reign for years." He closed his eyes. "It seemed to me that King Marcel liked having an advisor in his brother. In fact, after Giles told Marcel that he could track down Evelline, Marcel fully embraced the prince's vision."

"What vision?" David said, putting words to the cold, sinking feeling in Carine's chest.

Giles inhaled sharply. "I'll trifle with the details." He kept standing that way, back straight, face to the soldiers, as if on display, as if he had choreographed it all.

"What. Vision."

These weren't the boys she knew. Her friends loved each other and didn't show it, but they both knew it. These brothers hated each other, and they both knew it. And the entire change had unfolded before her eyes this morning.

"If you wanted to be involved in politics, you should have shown an interest sooner," Giles was saying, "but instead of aiding the kingdom through a leadership transition, you have been gallivanting around town in a costume."

His Majesty King David drew his sword and managed to stand.

A deep frown framed his mouth. His eyes did not flicker for one second from his brother.

Giles didn't startle. "King for an hour and the power has already gone to your head. What would you do with a kingdom anyway? You're naïve at best and stupid at worst." He opened both his arms to David, even as the king stepped closer with his sword out. It wasn't fair for them to fight with swords; Giles would beat him in a second. "You're my brother, David. I do love you. I always have. But you and I both know that between you and me, I'm better for the crown."

David let out a guttural scream, and lifting the sword high over his head, he hurled it off to the side.

Giles snorted. "What are you going to do now, David? Hit me?"

David didn't seem to hear. He lunged.

For a moment, they were fists, elbows, and velvet capes.

"Stop it," Carine wanted to say, but the words didn't make it out.

The king stood over his brother. Giles lay strewn over his indigo cape, legs sprawled out on the floor. There was blood on David's fist that dripped in one drop onto the white marble. David drew first blood. In the unspoken rules of their tussle, that was his victory.

But looking at a defeated Giles, David's eyes widened. He stepped back, catching his balance and his wheezy breath.

Only now could Carine see the large black stain on Giles' cheekbone.

Giles laughed drily, leaning back on his elbows as he perceived the mark through David's expression. "Would you look at that? We're both dead."

# 31

## DEATH OR GLORY

David wheezed labored breaths as his shoulders rose and fell.

"What have I done?" he whispered.

Nobody moved as the new king of Navafort fell to his knees. After a painful-sounding series of coughs, throughout which he watched his brother over his sleeve, David knelt at Giles' side. He opened his mouth to speak, but buried his head in his hands.

"In a week our kingdom will fall to the fauns," Giles said matter-of-factly. With no one left in their bloodline, the fauns would be next to inherit the crown.

Carine's hands covered her mouth. Not Giles too. Not both of them.

"…Or not," said Giles, rising to his feet. King David looked up at his tall younger brother from his puddle of remorse on the floor. It looked—perhaps it had even been designed to look—like David was kneeling to Giles. The prince turned to the soldiers, giving them a good look of the black spot on his cheek. It was large and unmistakable—there were bumps where David's knuckles had been.

As all looked on, Giles' lips moved ever so slightly. The black spot curled away, vanishing without the faintest line to mark it had ever been there. Prince Giles lifted his chin, as if to show off his clear, clean skin.

The soldiers murmured, transfixed.

David's mouth fell open. He struggled to rise to his feet, but could not.

Carine's stomach lurched. This was dark magic, mispronunciation as Didda had used. But unlike Didda, Giles had planned this perfectly. He used his power not to heal or protect, but for his own self-aggrandizement. Carine wanted to slap that arrogant grin off Giles' face. She wanted to destroy him.

But it made no sense. She loved Giles as a dear friend. How could he have come to this?

Prince Giles turned to Carine, his intense eyes filled with the delight of a perfectly executed plan. "If your father's blood runs through my veins, I hope that doesn't make us siblings."

Carine's teeth clenched. "You…" She couldn't say it. She couldn't picture Giles drinking some of Didda's blood. When Didda was dying and needing help, Giles was taking his power for himself. When Didda was suffering under his slavery to mispronunciation, Giles was gaining it too. How dare he destroy this legacy of her father? How dare he do this to David, to her? "How dare you?"

"Don't judge so harshly, Carine. Soon you'll be just like me."

Insolence! She spat toward him, regretting how far away they stood. "Don't speak to me."

"All this time?" David whispered to his brother, still on the floor.

Carine couldn't bear to see him that way. She couldn't bear to see him grovel at Giles' feet.

She marched over to His Majesty King David, grabbed him around his clothed waist, and helped him stand. He was careful, more careful than ever, not to contact her skin, but he could hardly keep his eyes off his twin.

Carine and David both understood, that with few exceptions, they were all each other had now.

"I couldn't well come out with it before the time was right," Giles said. "Besides, I needed time to practice the language."

David was standing, but couldn't bear his weight alone. Carine steadied him, grateful for the close semblance of a hug. She wanted to bury her head into her hands and cry into an embrace. For now, this would have to do.

A strange expression crossed David's face. "You healed yourself."

Giles lifted a brow. "I can heal. I can build. I can fight. All perks of the Gift of Calling. I always knew I was gifted." He flexed his fingers. "Now the world will know it."

David's voice was small, broken. "You'd heal yourself but not me?"

For the first time, Giles looked sincere, like he was sad about this too. "I want to heal you…"

Carine sighed conflicted relief. There was this tempting logic: if Giles was willing to compel anyway, he might as well use the dark power to heal his brother.

"…I'll heal you the second you renounce the throne."

At this, David's face blanched. He breathed heavily, wheezing. He was saying words, but Carine could barely distinguish them as she tried to keep him standing. So this was Giles' ultimatum: the crown or his life. Though, the way David saw it, both were his duty to uphold as gifts. "How can you say that? You're my brother. My *brother*."

"What about Carine?" Giles said, his voice even. "The one you're leaning on? She's in just the same position as I am, but you give her a free pass." He turned coldly to her. "You could have healed him days ago, but you let him suffer because you're afraid. You're the one who's letting him die. Some friend."

Carine shivered as tears blurred her vision of the indigo-caped, silver-plated prince. Part of her believed Giles was right, but another part remembered that there was good reason she chose never to compel. There was good reason to choose granddad's path over Didda's.

"Renald," Giles summoned.

"Yes, Your Majesty," the knight said, bowing as one bows to a king. This wasn't a challenge of David's authority; it was a takeover.

Renald pounded a staff twice, as if Giles needed something else to draw attention to him.

"Knights and soldiers," Giles said, spreading wide his arms as though he were in charge. "Padliot's army will be here today. They plan to destroy Esten, and you are far too few to stop them. Put your loyalty in me, dear soldiers, and I will deliver you. I will crush them, drive them back, and then you will take the rest of what is theirs. We will not let them destroy Esten, but rather will take vengeance on Padliot for what they have done to our villages. And after vengeance is satisfied, we will take whatever we want for ourselves. This is your choice, soldiers: death…"—he gestured to David, who hunched over, wheezed and rumbled a terrible cough—"…or glory."

No one spoke; no one dared move.

"Your Majesty," Alviar said, breaking the silence. He came to King David's side and provided a white handkerchief that David used to cough again.

Giles paid him no heed. "Destroy the army that approaches," Giles commanded the soldiers. "Destroy their troops here, then venture farther and take down Padliot. Take orders from me, as you will shortly, when my brother abdicates the throne."

David made a face of pain as he leaned over his abdomen. He handed the kerchief off to Carine. As Alviar led David away, Carine noticed something in the kerchief. She unfolded the cloth, careful not to touch anything that could infect her.

There was tar in the kerchief.

# 32

# THE PRINCE

Carine held back tears. Giles scoffed when he saw the tar, and with a snide smile directed the confused soldiers out to their battle stations. Before, they'd had time to seek a cure, but now, the tar signaled they were within a day of David's death.

Carine touched David's name with a blast of suffering, but nothing changed.

In her mind's eye appeared the Manakor word *ilvara*, which would solve everything if only she'd compel it to. Instead, she followed the king into the hallway and put her hand on his shoulder.

"We will solve this!" she cried, though she couldn't believe it herself. There was no time anymore. There was no hope.

"He would really let me die just so he can have the crown." David's voice was raspy and soft.

"I'm not going to let that happen," Carine said.

"Why didn't I notice he's had the Gift? He must have been compelling for a while now. How can I have been so blind?"

"He lied to both of us."

"He hid this from all of us," Alviar said, closing the Great Hall doors. His face was worn. "I don't know if you two realize what a danger he is now."

Carine's heart pounded as she thought of the damage that compulsion did to her father. "I think we have some idea."

"You understand, then, that tricking nature like that will, little by little, destroy his soul?" Alviar asked, ever the teacher.

"It makes him someone he isn't," Carine said. "He will become addicted to it."

"And worse," Alviar said. "Over time, the poisoning effect of compulsion isn't just slavery and numbness. Just as he calls nature by perversions of its name, so too will he forget and fail to recognize his own. He will lose himself in the chaos of his whims."

"No," David said, his jaw flexed. "Giles doesn't have whims. I thought compulsion made a person lose control, but it isn't like he lost himself. He knows exactly what he wants. He knows exactly what he'll do to get it. That's the scary part. Giles is in control. He hasn't cracked; he's let himself free."

Alviar bowed slightly. "My king, Padliot is fast approaching. Your brother has taken the troops, probably to fight."

"…At least that's a mercy," David said.

But Alviar continued to his question. "What would you have me do?"

David's voice was so quiet that Carine could barely hear him. "Let Giles lead the soldiers. For now, at least he and I both want to protect Esten."

"Very well," said the centaur knight.

"But Alviar," David added before the centaur left to accompany the army. "Do what you can, please, to save Giles. You are his teacher. Can you save him from compulsion? Save him from the fate you described."

Carine's heart ached. David, doomed to die or renounce by his brother's ultimatum, still loved Giles.

As Alviar left through the side doors, David's eyes welled with unexpected tears.

"Don't give up," Carine begged. "I won't."

"What can I do?" David looked up, lost, through long lashes. "My brother has betrayed me…If I renounce, he'll go on. And if I don't, he'll go on and I'll be dead. Checkmate. Giles wins. And if I stay true to my honor like the father I never met, then I'll die for my people. But Carine…I don't want to die."

"Good King David," Carine said, emphasizing every word. She smiled through her eyes and leaned in. "I haven't taken your name off my wrist since the moment I wrote it. Something has to happen."

King David shook his head, his expression hardening into determination. "Thank you, Carine, but I just heard myself speak like a coward."

"You aren't a coward. Not at all…"

"My father died a hero because he didn't abandon his kingdom. All those soldiers are going to their battle stations knowing they will likely die. And me? I am safe in here, protecting no one, but sobbing for myself."

"David…"

"I want to live and die bravely, Carine."

"What about me?" Carine asked, her voice squeaking. "You can't die. I need you. I need you in my life. I just lost my Didda, David. Don't let me lose you too."

David's expression went soft. "How could I go on living? How could I stay here having renounced the throne like a coward, leaving it to Giles who just showed how poor a judge of character I am? How could I walk through the streets and see their faces? How could I face my brother? Giles would think even less of me than he thinks of me now."

She hated to admit it, but she agreed with David. He could never forgive himself for abandoning his people to the monster that Giles was acting like, or for pandering to Giles' ultimatum, enabling him to destroy himself with his dark powers.

"He loves you now," Carine said, feeling like she were begging him to hold onto his life.

"Love and respect are different things."

Carine stroked the name on her wrist and let the pain surge. "Don't die. I'm trying…I'm trying not to let you."

She took a breath, pausing before saying this dreadful thing…

"You and I both know Giles has been right about one thing. If I say the word…I mean, I can heal you. I could…" She thought of her father, compelling himself to death. She remembered what she had learned on the way to the dragon.

She remembered Kavariel's flame. Her stomach turned; her word came out as a whisper. "…compel."

David pinched the bridge of his nose, eyes squeezed shut so tight she couldn't tell if he was crying.

Carine's heart pounded as she awaited his response. Even for David, compelling would lead her down the path of her father. She had seen what that dark magic did to Didda. She had heard what Alviar said would happen if the path continued. Even still, "I want to help you."

"Giles betrayed me," David answered, shivering and hugging himself. "Death is all around. I've never felt like this, Carine. Everywhere I turn, there's darkness. If you compel—even to save my life—you'll be part of it too."

After a momentary relief that he didn't ask her to compel, she was swept up in limitation. She had no idea how to heal him. She had nothing else to offer him besides the wishing she was already doing.

He wheezily sighed. "Could you do me a favor and take me up to my room, Carine? There's something I want to see."

# 33

# VOW

David's window was open, and a crisp breeze fluttered through, along with the sounds of ocean waves, passing gulls, and battle horns. Carine looked toward the smoke-riddled horizon. Padliot was close. David pointed out the few soldiers as they took their weapons and bows and found their stations. It was hours from battle, and tension hung in the air: Esten would be outnumbered, and its small army's leadership was in question.

"Do you need to lie down?" Carine said, shivering, turning away from the window and clearing papers and various other debris off David's bed to the cluttered floor.

David shook his head and forced an unconvincing smile. "It's not time for my deathbed yet." He beheld his cluttered floor, eyes wide and smile becoming real. "This is what I wanted to see."

David bent and picked up a child's shoe, the mate of the one they had lost on the ship. He held the object to his ear. His expression beamed joy.

"Listen," he said, offering the shoe to her.

This time, Carine accepted the wish object and put it to her ear. From the tiny sole emitted a most glorious music.

"It's the whale songs," David said proudly, nostalgically.

He bent again and picked up one of his own shoes: a leather boot Carine had engraved for him. It needed polishing and cleaning now that jousting training was over and especially now that he was king.

Even as he wheezed, David traced his cursed, weak fingers along Carine's engraving of the dragon's wing. He traced the image of his hand holding up the gullon blood to the dragon. He traced artistic tendrils of smoke and jagged dragon's teeth. He touched the healing pool, with a twinge of sadness, knowing it could not heal him from there. David's thumb touched the image of Giles, running behind them with a sword and torch. David's lips weighed into a heavy frown. "I miss him already."

But just as Carine struggled for a comforting word, David saw another object, this one on his bookshelf. "Look!"

It was the torch they had carried home with Kavariel's flame. This was the torch that had saved their kingdom from the Heartless Ones, a sign of their victory.

"I did right by my kingdom already," David told himself, easing onto the edge of the bed since his weary body was too fragile to remember wonderful things standing. Smiling, he brought the whale song shoe back up to his ear and smiled. "This life…it's beautiful, Carine. It's so good."

Carine saw his eyes fill with joyful tears and the first thing that hit her heart was jealousy. How could David say that? He was dying. Esten was in danger. Her mother was in danger. Her only other friend—if she was honest—had turned on them. The Death Dragon's Kiss had poisoned her life.

Carine's voice was small. "It's dark to me. Everything's dark from where I stand."

"You help me, Carine. You are a sign to me. You remind me of what's light and beautiful when everyone else has betrayed me…" The ease in David's expression dried up. "You won't compel, right?"

"Of course not," she whispered.

"Because I need you to stick with what you told me. You told me you'd never compel like your father did, like Giles is doing. Remember how we felt in the dragon's flame? Don't cheapen that."

"Don't worry," she said. "I won't. I won't compel."

He took a breath, wrapping his arms around his shoulders. Then, very slowly, not too harshly, he said as fact, "You've lied to me before."

"What are you talking about? The cloak? I only lied to save your life."

He raised his eyebrow, for a second almost resembling his twin. "Exactly."

"That was before. I wouldn't lie to you now. Never. And I wouldn't lie about the Gift and the call. I promise."

David clenched his jaw, eyes glazing over now as he looked at to his window. "I'm scared, you know. I want to be a hero like my father, but I'm scared." Carine's heart pounded. "I have avoided the darkness you feel by remembering beautiful things like the whale song, the dragon, and you…" He didn't meet her eyes. "But I feel it approaching. I feel it coming closer like Padliot's army or a black fog. I need a stronger guarantee than a promise."

Carine swallowed. "What's stronger than a promise?" She thought for a moment. "I can swear on something important."

"Stronger than swearing," the king said. "Make a vow." There was something powerful in his desperate intensity.

"But..." Vows were sacred, like marriage or allegiance to Navafort.

"I don't know what will happen at the hour of my death. I may waver. I may beg for you to cure me. I have to know you won't." His trembling hands pressed together. He looked at her like a beggar. A beggar in king's garb.

Carine shut her eyes. She had never made a vow. Her internal policy was to avoid them.

"I have to know that with more confidence than anything in the world. If you make a vow, I know you'll never compel no matter what I do."

When she opened her eyes, Carine was ready. She would never follow the wretched path that Didda and Giles had taken, the path that destroyed two people she cared about.

"I vow," she said, the words flowing purely and truly off her tongue. David sighed a breath of relief. His face relaxed; he smiled. "I vow never to compel."

"You meant it," he said, as though surprised.

"I wouldn't have said it otherwise."

David's shoulders hunched over his body as his strength dried up. His eyes met hers in true sincerity. "Thank you."

Carine placed her bare hand on the brown leather of David's glove. His thumb and first two fingers took her hand and squeezed.

King David closed his eyes and leaned over his knees. His breath was slow and gravelly. His lips were pale.

Carine needed him to stay alive. She needed him. He couldn't leave.

Without opening his eyes, David whispered three words that sounded both as natural as breath and as undeniably strange as the fact that he was king. "I love you."

Carine shivered in a way that felt both good and frightening. She wanted to tell David she loved him too, but the words were more difficult to speak than Manakor. Instead, she squeezed his hand tighter, begging him in her mind to hold on and keep living.

David squeezed her hand back.

But just as David's breathing became more labored, as he lay onto his mattress and succumbed to sleep in his weakened state, Carine's gaze fell on somebody moving about in Bastion Park.

It was Selena, the girl with glittering Manakor on her arms and a light around her neck.

Suddenly, something made sense.

# 34

## EMBER BEARER

Carine wrapped her old green cloak around herself as she clicked past the folk to the edge of the square. From up high, she had seen Selena slip into the well-house where Mom was staying in South Esten. It was uncomfortable to leave David in the place he called his "deathbed," but maybe this was the way to avoid that fate.

She should have understood the connection before. All this time she had dismissed Selena as David's fangirl, but she hadn't considered what the bright object on her neck might be, or what the writing on her wrists meant about her.

But when Carine entered Mom's well-house, she was not first to speak.

"You!" Selena said in her thick accent, smiling. "I have been looking for you."

Mom rushed forward. "Oh, my sweet Carine. I was so angry and scared last night. I didn't know where you were…but this morning, we heard about what happened. I am so sorry. I am so sorry for you, my dear. I know Prince David was your friend."

She wrapped her warm, maternal arms around Carine's shoulders and patted down her hair.

"Was?" Carine pushed her gently away. "He isn't dead yet, Mom." She wanted to add "and he loves me!" but restrained herself. This wasn't the time. That wasn't what mattered now.

A strange expression crossed Mom's face. "But…everyone's heard his highness Prince Giles is in charge now." She closed her eyes and bowed her head. "Excuse me… It's King Giles."

Carine scowled. "You heard wrong, and he is *not* the king. I'll explain later."

"Carine, I must apologize," Selena said. "When I followed you to the cave… I was such a fool! I misinterpreted some things…"

"That doesn't matter now," Carine said, to Selena's evident relief. "For now, I have to know: what is that thing around your neck?"

It was clear the question pleased her; a bright smile flowered on Selena's round face. The Manakor on her wrist sparkled as she reached up and touched the drawstring pouch that the light had shone through in the cave. "It's an Ember," she said, her voice low and reverent. "It is a piece of the Etherrealm. There is a tree as tall as a mountain that grows on the—how you say?—crack between this realm and the next. When its leaves fall through the veil into our world, the Ember Catchers catch them. As an Ember Bearer, it is my work to deliver them to the ones they were dropped for."

"So you are the one they've been asking for," Carine said, remembering the old man in North Esten crying out. "You *are* the Ember Bearer."

"Indeed," she said. "It is my life. It is the only reason I am here."

"Thank the flames," Carine said. "Thank the flames! You're the answer to all my wishing, I just didn't see it." All that mattered was the old man's question: Are you the one that heals?

"Wonderful," Selena said. "I know I am supposed to be here. I was pulled to this place by the call. But I do not know what I am supposed to do. That part has not been revealed yet." She gestured to the word on her left wrist as if that explained everything. Carine didn't have time to read it or ask questions other than this one:

"I have heard you are a healer. Ember Bearers are healers. That's what an old man was saying in..." She almost revealed her identity as North Esten healer. "...I heard someone say that once."

"It is the Etherrealm itself that heals. This Ember is a piece of it," Selena corrected.

"So that Ember was dropped for David?"

"Well...I thought it was. I have the Manakor on my wrists to help me." She turned over her wrists. "On my right wrist is my Manakor name, *Zhelena*. On my left wrist is the wish above all wishes, *viat*." Carine had heard that word before. Heino had described it when the Padliotians attacked. It meant submission to the Etherrealm. "To learn where I need to go or what I need to do, I wish on my wrists' tattoos. Then a desire, an attraction, pulls me to the next stage of my journey. When I finally got to Esten, I heard about the prince and thought about how long my journey had been, and thought that only for someone so important would I be brought here."

*Attracted to David.* Carine could laugh. It had been a linguistic misunderstanding. Selena had been trying to explain that she was called to him, to serve him as the Ember Bearer.

"Then go! Deliver it. And hurry. David doesn't have long; he coughed up the tar this morning. He only has a few hours now."

Carine tugged Selena's dark hand, but a strange expression crossed the girl's face. "I am sorry, Carine Shoemaker. I do not think you understand. I cannot heal His Majesty King David."

Carine frowned. Now wasn't time to quibble with technicalities. "Fine. Your Ember will heal him. Doesn't matter to me. Let's go."

Selena shook her head, black hair shaking. "No, the Ember is a piece of the Etherrealm—I told you that; it will do as it wills. But it doesn't heal physical sickness, only sickness of the soul. Otherwise, I would have physically healed His Majesty days ago."

Carine's smile faded. "So you're not a healer?"

"Not of the body."

"Then, this Ember won't save David's life," Carine's world was crashing. Her only hope was amounting to nothing.

"Not his mortal life. I'm sorry." Her eyes shone with sympathy. "I thought I was supposed to help him, but I still don't know why I have even come."

Carine covered her face in her hands. At this rate, she should have stayed with David. These were his last precious moments, and she had spent them seeking a dead end.

"But I have heard of a local healer," Selena said, eyes lighting up with a sudden idea. Carine looked up, too scared of another disappointment to hope. "He works in secret and is hard to find."

"Who?" Carine said, shaking. It was all she could do not to reach out and get Selena to tell her everything at once. "Why hasn't he come to the Bastion? Where is he?"

"I hear he is from the Bastion. He wears long hooded cloaks and a white scarf so that no one will know who he is."

Carine wanted to cry. Selena wasn't describing a male healer; she was describing Carine dressed up to write names in North Esten.

But as soon as Carine's hope died, Mom pointed out the window. "Look! There he is," she cried, pointing to a cloaked figure with a white scarf over his face. A crowd followed him at a reverent distance as he made his way to Bastion Park in the same garb Carine and David had worn to North Esten.

Was that David? Why was he back out in the streets? Had he come to find Carine?

Selena tugged at Carine's sleeve. "I may not be the answer to your wishes. Maybe this healer is."

# 35

## HEALER

Carine left Selena and Mom, and followed the cloaked figure into Bastion Park where a fearful crowd had already assembled. The ill cried for help and the well held pans and irons to defend themselves from the Padliotians. They could already sense their poor chances.

The healer moved swiftly, too strong to be David—unless Carine had despaired too soon that her wishes would remain unanswered.

But something about it wasn't right. If David were healed, why would he be in full healing attire a moment later?

As Carine looked up to the torch tower, her stomach twisted. "Selena," she said, "what happened to the torch tower's flame?" The dragon Kavariel's flame—which protected the kingdom from Heartless Ones, the flame for which Carine and David had risked their lives—was no longer burning at the top of the tower. "The enchanted sap still had time. The flame survives for a year on that sap."

"I do not know," Selena said. "Everyone was speaking of it last night."

"Are the kingdom's other torches out too?"

Selena shook her head. "I do not know."

"We'll have to find out," Carine said, mentally adding, "after we save David."

The cloaked figure stepped up the white marble steps of the flameless torch tower and turned to the crowd. His posture was perfect.

Carine pushed her way to the front of the crowd.

"He saved my life," someone was saying as they passed. Carine recognized a faun from South Esten whom she had wished for. She must have healed him when she was in the library. The folk didn't know Carine had been the one to wish for them, but she hadn't thought it mattered.

"My people," said the cloaked figure. A chill shivered up Carine's spine. She recognized this voice. It certainly wasn't David's.

Prince Giles took off his scarf, and the folk broke out into cheers. He didn't have to say anything else.

"Our healer!" someone shouted.

"Prince Giles healed my daughter," someone else cried, tears of joy in their eyes.

No. It hadn't been Giles. Carine was the one who had wished for them. That daughter was the first non-soldier Carine had wished for.

A man fell to his knees. Like trees in an earthquake, the others followed. Before long, only Carine stood standing.

Giles' eyes landed on Carine. He smirked and ignored her.

"I am your new leader," Giles announced, confident as ever. Carine glimpsed Renald with his announcement staff at the base of the stairs. "And I care deeply for my people. I have roamed these streets and already healed some with my power." *Liar.*

Giles met Carine's eyes and smiled.

"You have seen what I can do. You have also heard of Padliot's brutal attacks. Fear not, for under my leadership you will be protected." His voice softened.

Those who had knelt muttered among themselves.

"Does anyone here have the Death Dragon's Kiss? Stand, show yourself."

Prince Giles looked around. When Giselle and Elias' cousin stood, coughing, holding his hat, Prince Giles looked him in the eyes and said, "I will let you live, if you dedicate your life to serving me."

The boy nodded, not daring to make eye contact with his revered healer.

With a word hissed from Giles' lips, the mark disappeared.

The crowd reacted, startled and overjoyed. In the next few minutes, several more stood, begging to serve Giles in exchange for their health.

Carine's stomach turned.

"You can't do this," Carine said, voice quiet. But as though he were waiting for her to interject, Prince Giles smiled.

"Indeed," he said. "I can."

"His Majesty King David is the true king of Navafort," Carine said, her voice louder this time.

No one joined her. All held their breaths.

"I should hope that my subjects believe in me. I have your best interests in mind. For example..." Giles swept his arm over the black flower that lined the base of the torch tower and wrapped up the bottom third of its pillar. "This is the flower that continues to give us heartache and grief. Carine Shoemaker of North Esten, wouldn't you like to see me destroy it?"

Carine clenched her jaw. This was a trick. If she said no so he wouldn't compel, the flower could infect more people. If she said yes, which she wanted to do, it would be a sign she supported his coup, his betrayal, and the way he yielded his power.

"Wouldn't you?" he asked again.

Half the crowd rose to their feet; the other half bowed lower, some raising their arms in eager supplication. "Yes, King Giles!" They were already calling him king! "Destroy the dragon's plant for us! Save us!"

Carine's chest rose and fell.

"So you will not answer me?" Giles said, directing his question again to Carine. This time the crowd didn't hush to hear her answer. They shouted pleas.

"Save David," she said. It was all she could answer. Whatever happened, David needed to live.

Giles smiled. "I see my morality is of no concern to you."

She didn't answer; he was right. What a miserable creature she was, begging him to continue his perversion of nature so she wouldn't have to.

He didn't wait for her to speak. He muttered a word, his lips and eyes moving intensely the way Didda's had.

The trellis of black flowers that circled the base of the tower shriveled and shrunk, puffing into dust, leaving only a trail of soot.

The plant extended down to Bastion Park, and it shriveled, died, and puffed little by little. It met a fork in its stem where it went back to another offshoot. Folk stepped and clopped out of the way of this dying plant, rejoicing as they did so.

"Glory to Giles," they said, and it rolled off their tongues so much easier than "Glory to the Great Marcels."

"It didn't heal me!" someone shouted with raised arms. "The plant is dead but my mark is still here. Good Giles, I offer my allegiance. Heal me!"

"Of course it didn't," Giles said. "This plant only spreads the disease. I have prevented it from spreading further. You will do well to remember, my people, what I have done for you today and all along. Soon I will demand of you many changes and sacrifices. Your swift obedience will be necessary."

The crowd was silent; their eyes were dewy. This was what they wanted. They were eating out of the palm of his hand.

They didn't care if he was after the ultimate good or just his own plans. They liked his power. They adored him.

David's open window above the library overlooked the Park. Carine pictured him weakly sleeping on top of his covers, trying to breathe. She wished he wouldn't see this disturbing event. Giles' betrayal was complete.

Suddenly the chanting crowd turned and went silent.

At the base of the Bastion, where the thick oak doors served as the entryway, one of them opened.

Out stepped the young King David, barefoot and wheezing as he tried not to lean over his knees. But in his hand, tip dragging along the earth, was a sword.

And on his head glistened his crown.

# 36

## UNRELIABLE ORDER

"Fight me," David said, barely able to keep up his shoulders.

Giles guffawed. "Do you really think that wise, David?"

"Just..." he answered, shaking his head. King David closed his eyes, and when he opened them, walked labored step by labored step to the torch tower stairs. The crowd parted around him.

Carine launched herself toward them, reaching inside her drawstring bag.

At the base of the stairs, David lifted his sword, and taking a wheezing breath, picked himself up one step. He repeated, "Fight me."

Giles sucked his teeth, unsheathing his sword. "If you insist."

Carine pushed past the onlookers and broke through to the bottom stair as David took a second step up.

"Renounce, David," Giles said, voice even and clear. The crowd held its breath.

David didn't waver. "I'd rather die."

Giles sighed, placing his left hand behind his back and readying his sword with the other. He stepped down one stair closer to his brother. "I'd rather you not die. You're my brother, the only one I have left, really. I'd prefer you make this easy on both of us. But, it's your choice whether you work with me or not."

"Stop it!" Carine stepped up one stair.

"This is our fight," said David. He started to turn to her but must have decided against it; his movements were sickly slow.

"And what are you going to do? Fight to the death?" She marched past the true king, planting herself firmly between the twins on the stairs. "Would you really kill him? Giles, I'm asking you right now to stop all of this."

"Let me think about that," he patronized. "No. Not until you renounce, David."

The young king touched the crown as if double checking that he still had it.

"Stop it," Carine said, feeling the desperation she'd felt when begging Didda in his final hours to control himself, to stop using that perverted dark magic. Little good it had done Didda. "Let him go."

"You act like this is my fault," Giles said, sword still drawn, hanging out between them.

Behind and below her, David gasped and wheezed. The tip of his sword, raised a moment ago, had fallen to the stone step in front of him; he couldn't bear the weight of it.

"Do the right thing, Giles," she said. "Let it be."

"Or what?"

Carine shook. His question was a challenge. But she was ready: "I'll fight you." Opening her palm, Carine revealed the wishstone she had pulled from her bag. Inscribed in golden Manakor was the word for *order*, the same word that her granddad Jon, the heir of Firebrand, had used to fight his crazed centaur master.

The stone felt small in her sweating palm. Cool and unreliable.

"You'd trust pure Manakor now?" Giles smirked. "Look at where it's gotten you."

And with a flash of his tongue, in the language of dragons, Giles spoke.

# 37

# THE GOLDEN CROWN

Fire exploded within her. As Giles called David's crown off his head, sweat bubbled on Carine's forehead. Her nails dug into the heel of her palm as she clenched the word *order* with every ounce of her strength.

Her wish had no effect, except to tear her insides to shreds. She opened her palm, and the pain curled away.

The golden crown floated over her head, up to the younger brother.

Panting, taking another breath, Carine tightened her fist again.

This time, the crown fell with a clamor onto the stairs. It bounced down to David, who reached out and stopped its momentum, but took a moment to regain his strength.

As he did so, an increasing volume of a rhythm of marching armor took Carine's attention. Coming from the Bastion in full armor, led by a fully vested Alviar in indigo colors, were a hundred knights. Among them were many that Carine herself had healed, including Sir Leroy, the first success of the day.

Alviar directed his arm forward and shouted to the soldiers, "Battle stations." They fanned out, many marching toward the front gate, through which the Padliot army would have to come if they intended to invade. Sir Leroy led another group up ladders to the top of the wall where they would shoot down the enemy.

But as the soldiers marched, Alviar stood still, stuck like a rock in a river. His gaze followed his pupil and king, weak at the base of the stairs.

Carine's heart moved with gratitude as he broke from his plan, and—as the soldiers took their positions farther on—Alviar reached the bottom of the stairs. Carine saw his burned face and patriotic colors, and couldn't help but feel joy.

Alviar reached out and placed the crown on David's head. David was panting, cheeks ruddy and ill. He looked as though he could barely move and barely registered Alviar's approach.

"Who do you think you are?" Sir Alviar spat up at Giles.

Carine took a breath, letting the break from wishing restore her strength.

Giles didn't answer, and Alviar didn't insist. He pulled out his sword.

"No," the weak king said, stopping Alviar with a motion of his hand. "This isn't your fight."

"Your Majesty... You're my king," said Alviar.

David swallowed. "Then help me up," he said, voice cracking.

Alviar closed his eyes and obediently bowed, letting David wrap his feeble arm around his waist. As Alviar rose to help the king up the next stair, David's forehead rolled toward the knight and hit the centaur's chin.

David's head wobbled as he tried to get it to stay up straight. His arm trembled as he tried to point the tip of his sword up past Carine towards Giles.

But the damage was already done, and Alviar—without seeing the black spot—bowed his head reverently, accepting his new fate.

David was too frail to notice.

Giles stood still at the top of the stairs, where one could enter the base of the torch tower and climb the rest of the way up inside. He waited for David and Alviar as they climbed, his gaze flitting from them to the crowd, preparing his next move.

Carine couldn't bear to see David prepare to fight Giles in this state. All the courage in the world couldn't compensate for his sickness.

David may have told Alviar not to fight for him, but he never said that to Carine. She turned to Giles, wishstone on her open palm. "Stop this. I'm warning you."

Giles frowned. "What is it like, never knowing if your suffering will matter?"

Behind her, David answered. "The good... That's what will happen."

"Are you sure about that?" Giles said. But he didn't direct it to David; he was asking Carine. His fascinating eyes probed hers, and her breath caught. She had a doubt—the very smallest doubt, but still a doubt—that pronunciation would be best in the end. If good magic really would make the good happen, wouldn't David be healed?

It was as though Giles could hear her anxiety, as though he understood this crack in her defense.

David coughed into a tight fist in Alviar's strong hold. Carine had promised him she would stay true to what they knew about magic, about what was right and what was wrong.

Again, Giles called the crown.

Carine closed her fist and held fast to the wishstone, more determined now that he had preyed on her doubt.

As Giles compelled, her wishing became more difficult. With every word he spat, her bones ached deeper. Carine's knees shook; her face felt hot.

But Giles kept compelling.

Carine trembled. She braced herself on the white stone banister.

The crown, on David's head beside her, stayed still, and after a moment, the quick snaps of Giles' lips ceased as he conceded.

Victory!

But Carine could not enjoy it. She collapsed onto her hands and knees, the wishstone skipping away down the stairs. Her chest rose and fell as she caught her breath.

But Giles didn't let her.

He called for it again, simultaneously whipping his sword forward.

Carine raised her hand to stop it, but that did nothing. Gasping, she reached out, but the wishstone was too far away. Her arm was so heavy to raise.

The golden crown slowed as it floated past her head; Giles was toying with her.

Unable to reach the wishstone, she did all she could do: reached out for the crown herself.

The metal was cold in her grip, and the interference was enough to break Giles' concentration. She pulled the crown to her chest and turned to King David.

David's face was clammy and pale; his eyes were wide open as Carine feebly lifted his crown. His eyes flitted from Carine to Giles, and up to the sky.

Before she could place the crown on his head, a foreign bugle sounded outside the gates. The crowd shrieked and scattered.

As she set the crown onto his hair, David's tree-ring eyes closed. His head fell back on Alviar's armored chest.

Carine went numb. This was the fate of *Karin*, the lonely: to lose her best friends and everything else with them.

# 38

## THE MOMENT

"He's not waking up," Carine said, voice rising.

Alviar had picked David up into his arms and clopped up past Giles into the base of the tower. Giles, with a short look to the empty park, didn't object, but asked if he was alive as Alviar lay David down on a chaise where foreign diplomats sat when they visited Esten's unique torch tower.

Alviar touched the king's wrist. "His pulse is slow."

Giles stood with his hands behind his back. "He fainted, then."

"It appears so," said Alviar. "Regardless, these are his last moments."

Alviar and Carine leaned over David on the chaise. Carine's bare hand curled around David's gloved hand. Even through the glove, it was hot and moist.

At the door stood Renald. He had followed Giles like a loyal henchman. Carine couldn't bear to even look at Limly's brother. He was just as bad as David's brother. Irrationally, she felt Renald was even worse than Giles. It was like Renald was smug that Giles was betraying David.

David's eyes fluttered open.

"David! Thank the flames," Carine whispered. She kissed the leather of his glove.

But his eyes were wide. David didn't look himself; he looked small and scared. "The curse is pulling me," he whispered. "It's slow...but I feel myself freezing all over." He wheezed. "I'm chilling down to nothing. Everything's shutting down." His breath was short, but he wasn't gasping.

"I'm working on it, David. Don't lose hope," Carine said, untying David's Manakor name *Tavit* from her wrist. She did this with only one hand. In no circumstances would she let go of David.

"I'm not ready!" David said, eyes darting between hers. His breath was short, but he was not gasping. He turned to his brother, with a look of history that Carine had never seen. He said his twin's name with more depth than Carine had ever heard. "Giles. Giles, help me."

But Giles' response was cold. "Save yourself. Renounce."

"You can't," Carine said, reassuring David. He couldn't let the kingdom go to Giles, not after all Giles had done. She curled her fingers over the word in her hands, forcing all her energy into curing him. The blood sapped from her face as it at once felt cold and boiling.

"Don't renounce then," Giles said. "Carine can save you."

*I'm trying,* she wanted to say, eyes filling with tears. It wasn't working. Even as she held David's hand, his grip was getting looser. His hand felt colder, even through his glove.

There was a jolt of recognition: this wasn't working, but Carine *could* compel. She could will him to be healed and he would stand up straight, good as new.

David's lungs sung slow, soft wheezes that flowed past raisin-dry lips.

His wet, wide eyes met hers. "Don't." David's eyes stared up at the ceiling. His mouth fell open.

Carine clenched her teeth, doubling over David's name. It wasn't working!

Prince Giles stepped closer; Carine dropped David's hand and pulled out her awl.

"You are a coward," she growled, her insides searing. "You're letting your own brother die."

"Blame me all you want, hypocrite. Either of you can stop this with a word. You learned the word for health from Alviar." A smile spread across his lips. "Repeat after me: *ilvara.*"

Giles didn't will for his word to do anything so David remained still and slow, drifting toward death on the chaise.

Carine swallowed, staring down at the Manakor in her hand. A tear rolled down her cheek. "Alviar," she whispered, as the centaur wiped a damp washcloth on the king's forehead. "Why isn't it working? Why isn't anything happening?"

But Giles answered. "Have you considered that the Etherrealm knows it's best for me to be king?"

Carine shook her head. Lying, betrayal, ultimatums...this wasn't leadership. Giles was wrong, he was sick, like Didda had been.

"It's not that hard, Carine: *il-var-a.*"

"I'm afraid," David croaked. "Help me."

Carine's heart was wasted; David was begging her, and pain roared through her, but it wasn't helping. She was trying, but she couldn't answer his plea.

Giles raised his brows, arms crossed over his chest.

The breath was leaving him; his eyelids gave way to their weight.

Two desperate words gusted from his dry, parted lips: *"I renoun—"*

*"Ilvara! Ilvara!"* Carine interrupted.

Like a harsh wind, the Manakor settled in the silent room. A satisfying chill soothed the fire within. Where before had been desperation, now was stunned silence. Where before was haste, now was stillness. Where before was blinding pain, now was pleasurable relief.

Before there had been fear… now there was something else.

# 39

## THE SILVER CROWN

David's forehead shone with the sweat from his brow. Color bloomed back into his cheeks, and shiny clarity replaced the cloudy deadness of his eyes. His strong breath and the rustling of the chaise were the only sounds as King David hoisted his torso up on his arms.

Carine's heart soared.

Daring a glance down, David shifted his weight and rolled up his sleeve.

There was no mark; his skin was clean.

David's dark brown eyes flashed up at Carine behind long eyelashes. His gaze landed for only a second, but it was as though he were afraid to see her.

Carine wanted to hug him. They could hug now, since he was cured, but his posture, angled away from her, made her hold back.

Additionally, the Manakor names, which before had burned, now itched. The itching was turning to sheer scorching as Carine backed toward the wall and undid the leather fastens. The list of names fell to the floor, and Carine breathed deep relief. A cool calm settled in her bones.

"Glad to see you're feeling well, brother," Giles said, shattering the silence in a clear, confident tone.

David made the expression of one smelling garbage. Without responding, he leapt off the chaise as though he had never been sick.

A smile spread across Carine's lips, but David didn't share in her joy. In fact, as he straightened the crown and his royal vestments, he turned to Alviar to leave. Try as Carine might to catch his eye, she couldn't.

No wonder he wouldn't look at her; she had broken her vow.

...But didn't he understand that it was only once? Only to save his life?

"David..." she said.

He froze. His back bristled as he faced the door to leave. Instead of answering, his shoulders heaved, and he stepped one foot in front of the other to the door.

Alviar met her eyes with sympathy as he clopped one hoof at a time after his king.

But David never made it to the door.

With a hissed whisper from Giles, the golden crown lifted off David's head. David looked up as it hovered over him.

All at once the golden metal faded to cool silver and the red gems became blue. It hurtled into Giles' waiting hand even as the colors changed.

The youngest prince raised his eyebrows as he adjusted the silver crown. He turned to Renald.

"A little crooked, Your Majesty," said Renald.

Giles pushed the crown up with his left finger until it sat straight.

Across the room, by the door, David unsheathed his sword. The motion was stronger than Carine had seen in a week, more determined than even during the sword fighting competition that felt like so long ago. There was something beautiful about his strength, when moments before he had been on the brink of death.

But before Carine could intervene, David lunged at his brother. He yelled out with all the depth of the deepest wound.

A word from Giles was all it took to whip David's sword from his hand and rotate it. Pointing at David's chest the way Didda had done, the sword darted forward to impale.

Carine didn't have time to block David. But she didn't feel sad or scared at this, rather relieved. Because now she had the perfect excuse again, the perfect reason to do the thing that would cool the uncomfortable warmth rising in her. It wasn't selfishly that she did this, the logic went; she had no choice.

Carine had no time to whip out her ribbon shield or physically intervene in any other way.

Instead, a Manakor word spilled from her lips, splintering the sword where it hovered in the air. The metal shards sprinkled to the ground as debris.

Inside, Carine felt a good sensation, like a glass of water given to one in a sauna. Her discomfort died, dampened by this welcome breeze.

"You too?" His Majesty King David looked at her with slicing sorrow, even as the cool refreshment faded and discomfort grew again. His hair was messy, and his head looked surprisingly empty without the crown.

A pang hit her heart. His "too" put her in the same category of betrayal as his brother. "Of course not, David," she said, searching his eyes for the connection they'd had this morning. "I'm on your side."

"That hurts, Carine." Giles said, frowning under the jeweled silver that suited him in an eerie way.

David ignored him, meeting Carine's eyes intensely. His voice cracked. "You broke your word."

"I'm not betraying you," she said, not sure how to defend herself against her broken vow. "I'm trying to help you. I was trying to save your life." Suddenly his disdain filled her with indignation. "I *did* save your life. Twice."

David's head hung low. "Just stop, then."

Within, a horrid heat smoked her stomach. She had to touch her belly so as not to vomit. She knew instinctively what she had to do to stop the pain, but couldn't bear to have David see her do it.

"You ingrate," Giles said to David, baring his teeth and stepping up beside Carine in a way that made her uncomfortable, as if they were allies. Yet, she couldn't help but feel glad he put words to her feelings. "Can't you see she's been protecting you? And in exchange you do what? You scold her? What does it matter to you how she does something if it's for a good reason?"

"*How* matters just as much as *what* and *why*," David said, as if quoting one of Alviar's lessons.

Carine could barely stand. This absence of compulsion was worse than wishing for all the names on the leather. She craved it. She craved it more than air.

"I'm not using it for bad," Carine said, hardly able to get the words out.

David gave her the saddest, lowest expression she'd ever seen. "Isn't that what your father thought?"

The question hit her like an arrow. David was right.

"I won't use it again," she said, trying to get him to understand that those two events were only exceptions. "See?"

She reached down for the wishstone and gathered it in her bare hand. As soon as the golden lettering hit her skin, she let out a shrill shriek.

Before, the stone had burned like an ember. Now, it scalded like a red hot knife slicing her ice cold hand.

Manakor was painful before; now it was unbearable.

Outside, there was an unmistakable crash. Padliot had breached the gates.

# 40

## POWER IN WORDS

"Come on, Alviar," David said, drawing his sword. "Esten needs us."

Carine noticed that he hadn't included her on his team. She noted how he avoided meeting her eyes.

Giles laughed, compelling the doors closed. "You're not going anywhere until you renounce."

David gritted his teeth and twirled to his brother. "Still? Give it *up*, Giles!"

Before Carine could recover, Giles make a quick and sure command to Renald: "Arrest him."

Renald, obedient as ever to his "king," drew shackles from among his armor and went for David.

Carine gritted her teeth. David might not understand why she did what she did—she may not have understood it herself—but she wasn't about to let Giles imprison him.

It took all of her strength to stand up straight from where she had hunched over.

"Let him go, Giles," she said. Her voice went low, realizing how little she'd thought about Esten's poor chances against Padliot. "My mom's out there."

Giles grinned. "He won't renounce to save his own life, but maybe to save others. What do you think about that,

David? If you don't renounce, you'll be king over a vanquished people."

"You're bluffing," David said. "You told the soldiers you would lead them to victory. You told them you would protect them with magic. What will they think of you if you fail them?"

"They won't think of me. They'll be dead," said Giles.

"This is evil," David said, grasping the door handles. "Let me out."

Giles was silent. Instead, his henchman did his dirty work. Renald stepped forward, but Carine was quicker.

She yanked the ribbon from her hair, so her growing strands swept down over the back of her neck. Whipping the ribbon in a sharp circle, her arm buckled under the sudden weight of the shield that appeared.

Carine heaved the shield, throwing it as best she could. It knocked Renald back before any compulsion could stop it. But the delay was only momentary.

Giles compelled the shield aside, grating it across the stone floor.

Renald regained his composure and belted forward.

Carine couldn't muster any strength to move. The pain was as though her blood were lava, melting the veins from the inside. Her hands and chest shook uncontrollably. She wept, neither from pain nor from sadness, but from lack of control.

Her hands, once balled into fists—though half a second ago, it felt like ages—were now limp at her side. She fell to her knees and the cool of the stone floor met her cheek and arm.

Her teeth clattered.

She was on fire. Burning. Not even dying—ending.

Somewhere swords were clashing. In the flash between blurred blinks, a centaur was fighting a knight. David stood behind Alviar, watching not the fight, but Giles.

"Is this how you want it to be?" a voice said. After a moment Carine realized it was Giles speaking.

And he was right.

She knew what would make her body stop shaking. She knew what could restore the peace of an easy breath. Even her tongue craved a word that wanted to be spoken.

Any word.

Any Manakor word would do.

"What are you doing to her?" said a voice. David.

A cool voice: "Nothing. It's her refusal to speak again that dooms her." Even his suave voice promised relief. If only she spoke as he did, she would be okay.

The cool of the floor transferred to her forehead as she rolled over. Carine pressed her palms against the floor. Her right hand pulsed where she had stupidly touched that Manakor word.

Everything that had happened felt like so long ago.

This wasn't the fire of Kavariel's flame, or the fire of pronunciation; this fire felt blue, the hottest hot.

Her ears rang.

The floor reverberated as Alviar fell; Renald slapped cuffs around King David's wrists.

Her heart was a slow, loud drum. Her neck ached as she watched. She felt as though she were reaching out to stop

Renald, but her hand was far too heavy to lift. Her face felt chill. She wanted to vomit.

Giles was speaking. She couldn't hear him, but the idea was perfectly clear:

Giles hadn't gotten David's renunciation before. He would get it now, even if it meant submitting Esten to a bloody defeat. He would let folk die. He would lock David in the dungeon. He would amplify his power. Giles would do whatever it took to see his designs fulfilled.

Carine's head swirled.

Her lips welcomed the tasty word.

The searing stopped. Lava at once cooled to normal blood. Her hearing at once cleared. Her strength and control were restored. The sweetest, most beautiful serenity replaced her discomfort. A single breath was a like a whiff of roses; to step up off the crushed earth was as light and easy as walking on clouds. Compulsion or not, she needed it.

Carine stood tall as Giles' sword slid from its sheath and sailed across the room into her waiting hand. Meanwhile, Alviar's mark disappeared and the crown flew back to David.

A smile spread across Carine's lips. Her heart lifted inside her cool, comfortable chest.

"Let him go," she commanded Renald, feeling the ease of her words. Speaking was easy: commanding in her native tongue and compelling in the language of the Etherrealm. Everything was natural to her.

Renald didn't listen. He didn't turn, or perhaps not fast enough. No matter.

With a thrust of the sword, she sank the blade under Renald's arm and impaled him.

Renald's breath caught. He froze.

David froze as well, his gaze transfixed on Carine's face. She shot him an unreciprocated grin as she whispered the shackles off her friends. They would win this. Things would be okay.

Renald hunched over. David reached for him, as if to help him.

"Let's go," Carine said to David. This was only the beginning. David would regain the trust of his people. He would do right by Navafort, and Carine would help him.

Alviar rose to his hooves.

"Come on, Alviar." Carine drew the sword from Renald's side, ready to toss it back to Giles in triumph. Her shoulders were light; there was a spring in her step.

But the blade came out clean.

# 41

## RENALD

The moment the blade came out clean, Carine's head felt light. Her face went hot. Heat rose slowly in the rest of her body. It was happening again.

"Surprise," Giles said, teeth gleaming. He stood tall and sure, unfazed.

"An Eldrin blade?" she asked, though her hilt looked nothing like the four Eldrin swords.

"Better," said Giles. "Guess again."

There was only one other reason a normal blade could pierce a person and they wouldn't bleed. Carine's heart pounded. "Renald's Heartless?"

"It was an experiment," Giles said. "I found Renald sick and dying, after you failed to heal him."

"You extinguished the flame," Carine said.

"The whole thing worked out better than I could have hoped. Wouldn't you agree, Renald?"

The knight bowed. As different as Renald was from Limly, they shared the trait of loyalty, though in Renald it was sickening.

"I can see what he sees…hear what he hears. It's incredible, really."

David's face contorted. "You ate his heart?"

Carine's stomach turned. Her teeth clenched as she tried not to picture Renald cutting out his heart like others had done for the dragon Luzhiv, and Giles...eating it. She understood now why Renald had had a knife in the hallway. She wanted to vomit.

"This mark won't kill me now," Renald said.

Now that she was looking, Carine could see that his skin was lighter, and the mark of the Death Dragon's Kiss was still there. Giles hadn't really healed Renald; he preserved his existence, though now the man could not feel. Carine could barely look at Giles. Since he had eaten the heart, did that mean he had the power to choose—at any moment—if Renald would live or die? Could he control Renald the same way the disobedient dragon Luzhiv could control the Heartless Ones? "King Giles saved my life."

"There is no King Giles," David said.

"But if you don't renounce," said Giles, "there will be no Esten."

"Arrgh!" David screamed, releasing anger in an open-mouth guttural yell. "I hate you. There were times I thought I hated you before, Giles, but now I know what hate really is."

David whipped the door open, letting in screams as the townsfolk felt the approach of the Padliotian army. The crowned king looked out into his withering city, wind whipping against his healthy face, billowing through his crimson cape.

"It'll be okay, David," Carine said, confident she could claim victory. Giles and Renald could pull all the stunts they wanted, but she had a power they couldn't tap.

David studied her face, his eyes wide and chest angled back.

"It'll be okay," Carine repeated, reaching her arm out.

King David of Navafort jerked his hand away, and turning as though from a foe, he pulled out his sword and stepped into the war.

"David!" Carine called after him from the torch tower steps. But as he and Alviar raced to join Sir Leroy and the other soldiers, the wind drowned out her voice.

"Let them go," Giles said at her side, unconcerned by the battle about to rage.

Carine wasn't welcome to flee with David; that much was clear. And as much as she desired to go with him anyway, even more overwhelming was the inclination to compel again, to speak one of those sickly sweet words that cooled her within. Even already, as silence settled over the room, gross warmth filled her.

"But what about…" Renald began, but Giles interrupted him with a raised finger.

"Easy, Renald. Everything will happen at the opportune moment. Carine, don't worry about David. He'll understand in time."

Carine pressed her fingertips to her temple. Her insides were screaming, and all she could think about was David heading into certain death, along with Mom who was out there alone.

"Where's my shield?" she said, and then saw it on the floor. She reached out her arm and compelled for it using the closest Manakor word she could think of. It sailed to her waiting fingers as cool pleasure relieved her.

"You're unpracticed, but I will teach you," Giles said, his voice kind. "Try using your hand to amplify the power. Eventually you'll reach a level of mastery where you won't need to mouth the words. A flick of your wrist or a nod will do. I'm working on channeling the Manakor through my eyebrow." He smiled a little, watching her from the corner of his eye.

At first Giles' betrayal had saddened her, but now just hearing his voice made her sick.

"I can stop the burning," Giles said. "It threw me too when I first engaged my power. Is that where you'd like to start?" He reached out to her shoulder. "When you breathe in…"

"Don't touch me." Carine swatted his hand away, unintentionally opening the doors behind her.

A shiver ran down her spine as she realized that it was her own magic that had swung them open. Outside, folk were running through the park. Confused yells rose into the tower like smoke.

Giles raised a brow and stood. "When you inhale, imagine exactly how you want the world to be. I see you're getting close."

"Stop it," she said, bracing herself for the outside. "Stop teaching me. Stop acting like we're in this together."

Giles' face fell. "But we are. Without me, you're alone. Who else can ever understand you? Who else exists with the Gift we were given?"

"Given?" Carine's voice broke as the question burst like water through the mental dam that had kept her from dwelling on it. "You weren't given this. You took it. How could you, Giles? How could you drink my Didda's blood?"

Inside, Manakor ached to be spoken again.

"At the time I didn't know he was your father," Giles said.

But it didn't matter. None of it mattered.

She turned to the doors. With a punch at the air and compulsion in her lips, the doors flew open into the wind.

## 42

# BATTLE AT THE GATE

"David," Carine shouted, cupping her hands around her mouth. The wind swallowed her voice.

Padliot soldiers streamed through the gates on horses laden in orange armor. David was too close to them to use his preferred weapon, the bow. He and Alviar ran forward with swords out toward the oncoming army. King David's golden crown glimmered in the afternoon sunlight; his crimson cape whipped about in the fierce wind.

The slapping cold air made Carine yearn to compel again, to cool her heating insides.

But she was briefly distracted even from the sickening warmth, for the Padliotian soldiers were close enough now to see. The first line of soldiers was shouting and full of confidence, blades up as they faced the few remnants of Navafort's army in Esten.

The Padliotians were coming by the dozens. Behind the destroyed gate were more strong Padliotian menfolk, and behind them, where the soggy marshland turned back into solid land, were hundreds of soldiers in stark formation. These foreign troops had gained victory after victory, a story told by their high shoulders and bloodstained armor. Dirty smoke marked vanquished towns that had been ransacked or destroyed on the army's trek.

"David, stop!" Anger replaced worry: Anger that Esten was under siege at all. Anger that David wasn't listening. Anger that she had saved his life without thanks and now it was in jeopardy again. Anger that despite her Gift, she felt powerless. The anger roared within like the horrid heat inside. It soured like poison and uninhibited like wine.

Esten's brave few fought valiantly, but not enough to prevent a half dozen Padliotian riders from cantering down the alley toward King David and Alviar.

"Stop!" Carine cried, fuming, but this time she wouldn't let David ignore her.

Pivoting toward the Bastion, she called forth the only defense she could see: the iron gate that led into the castle. Compelling it from its position on the ground, Carine willed the gate to take its place between the soldiers and David.

She would not let him fight and die. Not now. Not like this.

The Bastion's gate rose several feet, soaring over the heads of the few that still stood and ran about, desperately seeking a plan with their city under siege. As it flew over them, Carine heard a Navafort soldier fall off the city wall. She broke concentration for a moment, a mistake.

In the moment of lost focus, the flying gate dipped low. Carine refocused, steadying the compulsion with her hand, but not in time to prevent cries as a few Esteners dropped under its weight. She did not see their faces from where she stood, but for the moment it didn't matter.

Carine concentrated on her aim; the gate hurtled past David and jammed itself between two buildings. And only just in time... As soon as the dust settled, David and Alviar reached the cold iron bars. The Padliotians reached the other side.

Carine stepped forward as the cool sensation of Manakor allowed her to relax.

David sheathed his sword and fired an arrow through the gate, trembling as Carine came near, shoulders rigid. He refused to face her. Carine was at the end of the street, within a stone's throw of him, but even though the wide-eyed Padliotian soldiers had pulled their startled horses back from the bars, crowned David did not turn.

An enemy soldier recovered from his surprise. He turned to Navafort's king, pleased, no doubt, by the idea that he might slay the ruler himself. He switched to his bow and launched the arrow at David's chest.

The shaft had no chance to strike.

Carine compelled the arrow, this time more easily and smoothly than she had compelled the gate. Turning it around, she speared it into the Padliotian's shoulder at the weak point in his armor. The Padliotian fell, attached to the horse at the stirrups.

David finally turned. Carine's heartbeat was steady and her lips were relaxed as tense David met her serene gaze. Despite the enemy army at his back, he backed up to the gate, as though preferring their proximity over hers.

Carine lifted her chin. Somewhere in the back of her mind was sadness that David's evident fear was not the reaction she wanted from him. But foremost, and compounded by the winning sensation of compulsion, was a satisfying validation: David—and no one else, for that matter—could ignore her.

She didn't have time to dwell on it. The Padliotian soldiers had solved the problem of the gate: within a moment, ten soldiers had rounded the building and cantered down the next street. They charged, swords drawn, intent on the prize: the king.

Carine spoke a word, and the ten soldiers fell down dead over their horses and onto the street. Their swords clattered to the cobblestone.

"What are you doing—?" David started, horror transformed to anger.

But there wasn't time.

Behind the gate was another line of soldiers, and they hadn't seen what had happened to their front line.

The sickly sweet Manakor fell like rain from Carine's lips; the next line of Padliot's best fell dead at Esten's door. Horses ran off into Esten's streets, empty saddles and all.

As the wind raged, the third line of Padliot's soldiers paused.

One soldier leapt off his horse and bolted, tripping into the marsh as he abandoned his rank. Carine smiled.

The others, spurred to courage by his cowardice, raised their swords.

Carine, with a word, stripped the blades from their grasp.

"Stop!" begged a female voice behind her.

Carine turned, teeth gritted, her hand raised to hold the swords in the air, aimed at the soldiers' chests.

The girl was Selena. Her black hair fell behind her as she peered around the building behind Carine. "You do not have to do that."

Carine looked at the swords raised up over the soldiers. She felt the sickening warmth of withdrawal filling her insides. She saw David's hopeful look dart to the uninvited girl behind Carine and wanted to scream.

Keeping one hand raised, she turned to the Ember Bearer who didn't heal, who had come and interrupted everything—including this—and swept her hand down. As Carine's hand swept over the building behind Selena, compulsion ran through her fingers. White South Esten limestone cracked and crumbled in the surrounding houses. Selena shrieked and ran as chunks of the building hit the ground with clouds of white dust.

Carine turned back to the enemy.

Padliot's soldiers knew what was coming. Their own swords pointed at their chests, they abandoned their ranks and pulled back. The effect of their retreat was like dominoes on the others. Row by row, they pulled back, at least on this side of the marsh. Their capes and the rumps of running horses were all Esten could see.

Padliot had retreated, at least for now. Time would tell how the hundreds stationed on dry land would react to the survivors' reports. No matter; if they came back, she'd be ready for them.

Carine's heart pounded. She wanted to smile for defeating the front lines, but there was something wrong in everything...in the way David was looking at her, in the blood on the street beside her, in the echo of Selena's scream, and in the eerily triumphant song of compulsion that resounded in her spirit.

*Clap. Clap.*

Behind her, Renald clapped haughtily.

"Go find Giles. We have nothing to do with you anymore," Carine said.

Renald smiled. "Fine, just as soon as the boy renounces."

"I won't renounce," David said to Carine's delight. This was the first good sentence she'd heard from him since he left the tower.

Renald wasn't as impressed. "I'm on strict orders from my master to get his brother's renunciation and crown, or to bring him back in irons."

Carine gritted her teeth. "You'll get none of those things. David's not going anywhere with you." She tossed him a glance, happy to be a team again. But David looked anything but her teammate; he angled his body away from hers and held up his sword as though still in battle. It slanted toward both Renald and Carine.

"Don't compel again," said David. Carine ignored him.

With a word, she pulled a door off its hinges and hurtled it at Renald. He destroyed it and retaliated *zhileam* ("in the name of Giles"), launching a stone from the limestone rubble toward Carine, even as he stepped forward with the irons in hand.

There was victory in the compulsion; she felt it in her veins. She would beat Renald. She would protect Navafort yet again. They would call her Esten's Shield, and would crown her with flowers one day each year. They would tremble in awe when she walked down the street, and everyone would know her name.

"Don't," David repeated, this time with deadness in his voice.

Carine launched another attack, if not to kill—she didn't quite know how to sever the link between Renald and Giles without a dragon's flame—then at least to stop him. Renald retaliated. They went on like this for a minute or two until King David stepped close to Renald.

"Stay back!" Carine called, but David did not.

"Look out!" Alviar called, but David didn't listen to Alviar either.

He went up to Renald, took the irons from his hands, and clasped them around his own wrists. "If Giles wants me so bad, take me to him."

Carine uncomfortably stopped compelling. "What are you doing? Giles isn't like he was before."

As Renald led him back toward the Bastion, David answered, "Neither are you."

Carine stood up tall as Alviar took his place beside the shackled king. "I'm trying to protect you. I'm trying to do what's right."

David's face contorted. "Don't you remember anything we've been through? I trusted you."

Carine's soul cried out to compel again, to save David from the chains he chose.

She took a step after him.

But David spat at her feet. "Don't follow me. Don't come with me anymore."

"David…" Carine's heart ached.

But he turned, hanging his head under the gleaming crown. The Heartless One led him and Alviar back to the boy he used to call brother, in the castle he used to call home.

43

# NO WAY BACK

The only Esteners in Bastion Park were the two that Carine had hit with the gate, and—hoods flopped over their heads—they looked ready to bolt.

The last woman was struggling to stand. Her hood fell back as she pushed herself onto her hands...

It was Mom.

Mom's eyes widened as she beheld her Manakor-whispering daughter. There was blood in her greying, unkempt hair.

"Mom," Carine said. Mom tried to rise to her feet, but stumbled again. Wiping an unwanted tear from her cheek, Carine ran to her mother.

Mom was holding her blood-matted head as she leaned over her knees.

"Mom..." Carine's voice wobbled. She wanted Mom to tell Carine everything would be okay. She wanted Mom to hold her. Inside, Carine's heart itched with heat.

Mom's beautiful blue grey eyes did not hold a tender mother's love, but rather the terror of a helpless animal.

Mom stepped back.

"I'm so sorry," Carine said, compelling a word of healing that immediately fixed Mom's wound. Carine's insides cooled. "I didn't mean to hit you. I didn't know it was you…I lost control. And David hates me now."

But Mom said nothing. Instead, she stepped back again, clutching her skirt with bloody hands. After a second, she turned and ran.

"Mom," Carine called as the footsteps faded. "Mom! It's me!"

The woman never looked back.

A breeze played with Carine's hair and the hem of her surcoat. She stepped back into the empty park, not daring to follow either of the ones she loved who didn't want her. She wanted to leave Esten and never come back, but exiting the city's gate would mean walking past more blood she had spilled.

Carine clenched her jaw and turned to the torch tower. Less than an hour before, she had defended David from his brother on these steps; now she flew up them, skirt in hand. Inside the tower, she found the dark interior stairwell and wound her way up, up, up.

Panting at the top, she walked out onto the empty torch plate, where enchanted sap-covered logs no longer burned with enchanted fire.

At her feet was all of Esten: the Vualtic Ocean behind her, Bastion Park empty beneath her, the Bastion beside her. On the city wall were still a few knights, stationed in case the thousands of troops across the marsh returned. Padliot's orange flag waved, and all the soldiers still faced Esten. They hadn't turned back, but honestly, Carine didn't care.

Mom raced across the bridge back up to the Grunge, fleeing the relative safety of South Esten for a place that would feel like home. Carine hated Mom for that. She hated David for fleeing her too. He would be somewhere in the Bastion now, listening to Giles' abuses, perhaps renouncing the throne despite everything she'd done.

She wanted to rage a tornado through Esten. She wanted to destroy her little hovel of a home to which Mom had retreated without her.

The warmth of withdrawal retreated as she formed a new will inside her. Stretching wide her arms at the edge of the limestone plate, Carine compelled dark clouds to gather and let them release their seas.

As the rain pelted down, she spoke another Manakor word: the iron gate that had blocked David's exit warped into an ugly shape. She looked down at the limestone that had broken off buildings when she was fighting with Renald and hissed Manakor until it all turned to dust.

Then, looking out at the orange army which had begun a slow second onslaught, Carine stretched out her hand. She yanked the bridges out from beneath the horses on the marsh. She swirled the rain into a terrible torrent.

The soldiers pressed down and continued, but with the mere desire of her will, Carine lifted up the marsh grass like a carpet and rolled it over them.

The horses turned in panic, throwing riders into the water below. Even from here, she heard their shouts and whinnies as they pulled back. This time, the thousands turned in panic. This time, they fled toward the trees with no intention of ever returning. Willing to live, they fled back to Padliot, and Carine chased after them with compulsion until they disappeared into the distant forest.

Carine's words flew out in sloppy wet hisses, her teeth together and sharp, her blood boiling, but her insides comfortable. Better than ever, in fact.

Such was her focus on the army that the rain had stopped. Esten was quiet.

And there at the top of the tower, Carine panted for breath, all by herself and drenched.

Carine shivered and wrapped her wet cloak around her. She sank to the floor of the torch plate and looked down at the Bastion.

Inside, heat was rising, and to protect herself from the pain she muttered the first word that came to mind.

An azalea, obeying her, bloomed from the limestone at her foot.

Carine pressed her dirty hands to her face. She had compelled to protect David, just as Didda had done for her. Was she a slave to this power as he had been?

"I'm not him," Carine told herself, even as she itched to compel the bloom back into the stone. She shook her head and stood.

Didda had had a choice; so did Carine.

She had compelled, just like Didda. But unlike Didda, she would stop.

Right this minute.

Inside, the discomfort of sick flames fumed through her. It wasn't the good pain she'd felt when wishing for Esteners to be healed; this was a violent, antagonistic pain, like that inflicted by someone who hates you.

It didn't last long.

To Carine's shame, after only a few minutes, when it was all she could do to resist vomiting, when no one was around to help her, and when she couldn't even cry out due to the pain, she compelled; the azalea disappeared into the dirt.

Carine curled up against the limestone statue of the dragon's head and tried again.

The sickening pain mutilated her within.

Not too long ago, Carine would have trusted another method. In fact, she would only have used that method.

Taking a stone, she etched the Manakor word for protection into the floor. It was the closest word she knew in Manakor for "help." Wishing this way, even if it hadn't healed David, had healed dozens of sick Esteners. It had protected her in Wyre from robbers and the dragon's flame. Wishing was powerful, and it was good.

If anything could help her, this could.

Carine slammed her bare palm against the now-golden word. A clean, bracing fervor consumed her.

But when it met the coolness of compulsion, a worse pain took hold.

Carine jerked her hand from the wall and backed away.

The warmth subsided but the searing pain did not let up until she compelled the azalea to bloom again. Carine curled up against the cool dragon jaw and cried.

And as tears speckled her cheeks, Giles must have uttered a word, because the Bastion changed form. At once, the ground below rumbled and a cloud of dust filled the air. Carine looked down on the Bastion as its great brick walls tore from the castle and hovered in mid-air.

The rooms inside were exposed: the throne, the dying potted palm plants in the throne room, the dragon skeleton on David's ceiling, the books in the library…like blocks, the walls separated. Furniture slid from tilting floors and remained floating there in space.

Without pause, Giles' new structure assembled itself. Room stacked upon room in continuous assembly until Giles' Bastion Tower was taller than the torch tower. Its rooms, unequal in size, were like precarious rocks stacked one over the other. Following normal rules of physics, the rooms should have crumbled and fallen, but Giles' power kept them up.

The tower cast a long shadow over the carved marble dragon she sat beside.

Before the walls went on, Carine glimpsed new stairs that ran outside from Bastion Park to the top. Giles' room, redesigned, crowned the top floor. His room had pillars around it, but no wall and no ceiling except a circular frame that rested on the pillars.

Balanced on top of the impossible structure was the throne, which sailed through the air, undoubtedly in response to Giles' compulsion.

Carine shivered and hugged her arms to her chest. She had the power—miserable though it was—to climb the tower's stairs and stop Giles, but David didn't want her help. Even worse, she hated herself for using her father's Gift this way at all.

She was alone in Giles' shadow, clinging to the stone dragon's teeth, and certain of one thing:

There was no way back to the way things were before.

# 44

## KAVARIEL'S CHORUS

Light footsteps in the stairwell made Carine's hair prick up. She sat up, calling to mind Manakor words she could compel if necessary.

Carine saw the brilliant light before she saw Selena's round face.

The Ember in the drawstring pouch on her neck shone brilliantly in the dark afternoon. The building Carine had destroyed beside Selena had scratched her face. Mud, building dust, and blood marked her foreign cloak.

Selena emerged from the stairs, carefully checking Carine's expression.

"Stop following me," Carine said from where she'd curled up at the dragon's jaw. She needed to compel again, so she whispered a quick word and bloomed another azalea, hating herself.

"Carine. I was wrong. I misunderstood everything."

"Leave me alone."

"I will if you want me to…" Something in Selena's tone made Carine hold back her retort. "But…I have discovered the reason I was called all this way. I don't know why I didn't see it all along. You already know I'm not here for King David, at least, not directly. The Ember…it's for you."

Carine's chest tingled. Selena was untying the drawstring pouch around her neck. She took out the glowing Ember.

Carine was hot with the need to compel again. She didn't dare to breathe, but watched the bright round Ember approach her on Selena's fingertips.

Carine shirked back. Now that David had spat on her and Mom had rejected her, Carine would have nothing if she lost her power.

She groaned, causing the azalea to suck back into the earth. It responded to her compulsion as other azaleas had responded to Didda's.

Fire whistled through Carine's insides. "I'm sorry for hurting you." She looked away, unable to bear Selena's response. Carine's plea came out quieter than a whisper: "Help me."

Before she could look up, Selena sank down beside Carine and put her arm around her shoulder in unexpected tenderness. She rolled the precious Ember onto Carine's fingertips.

"You make the motions of one at a funeral," Selena instructed.

The Ember felt light in Carine's fingers, like a coal. But it was so bright she could barely look at it.

Following Selena's instructions, Carine first touched the Ember to her forehead, which seared like nothing else. *It's a trick*, she feared inside. Her instinct was to drop the Ember, but this searing wasn't like withdrawal. It was a different pain: suffering the same way she had suffered when all those people were healed in North Esten. It cleaned her out, made her feel whole again.

Carine would have wanted Didda to accept any possibility that could have healed him, and he probably would have resisted, just as she wanted to resist.

But she would not do that.

She wished with all her heart that it wouldn't be. She wished to be rid of compulsion, to be clean of it.

Carine touched the Ember to her lips, and instead of intensifying the pain, as Carine expected, all the pain vanished. In its place was a depth she had only experienced in intimate conversations with her parents and friends. A beautiful silence reminded her, for some reason, of the chorus in Kavariel's flame.

At once she was more at home than she had felt in ages.

She took a sharp breath. These motions were like the motions one made for a dying soul, and Carine felt that her addicted, compelling self was dying, as the Ember brought her back to life.

The final touch was over her heart. She brought the Ember down on her surcoat and pressed the Ember close, hoping for even more of the beautiful, healing silence that came when the Ember touched her lips.

Instead, like a wind, it all vanished: the pain, the silent chorus, and the Ember from her fingers.

"It's gone," Carine said.

In place of the Ember was peace. Carine had energy and strength. She wasn't Didda; she was new.

Selena pressed her hands deep into her pockets and stood. "That's my mission; to bring the Ember to those who need it. To follow my call to them. I was afraid I'd done something wrong…"

Carine stopped her. Standing, she wrapped her arms around Selena and lifted her up, feet almost leaving the floor. Never had she had such a good female friend. Never had she been so cruel to anyone who responded with exactly what she needed.

"You'll need better boots for your journey home," Carine said. "I'll make you some."

"Before I leave…" Selena said, frowning at Giles' tower construction, "there is something I must say in good conscience. Prince Giles can't be king of Navafort."

Carine nodded soberly. "I know. And as long as David doesn't renounce, he won't be."

Enough time had passed—Carine should have suffered withdrawal—but no warmth tortured her. She was normal again.

Carine straightened her shoulders and checked her shield hair tie. It would be difficult, but Carine would free David.

Without dark magic.

And this time, it wouldn't be for him. This would be for Navafort.

"So," Carine said, grinning. "Are you still attracted to David?"

Selena hit her head. "Is that what I said? I realize what you must have thought. No, I was talking about my calling…"

"I know. My point is…did you just want to warn me about Giles or do you want to stop him with me?"

Selena looked taken aback. "You want me to come?"

"You say there's power in your wishing. We'll need all we can get."

# 45

## COMPELLED STEPS

Carine and Selena descended the torch tower and found the base of the Bastion Tower that Giles had built.

The new Bastion Tower didn't have a normal staircase made of wood or stone, but stairs made of a hodgepodge of materials from the Bastion that Giles apparently hadn't considered necessary in his new structure: hardback books, planks from walls, and old wooden drawers. There was no solid backing to the staircase, nothing that held everything together. Instead, each object floated a few inches above the previous one, held up—it appeared—by compulsion.

Carine stepped doubtfully up each stair. The books and drawers, however, did not shake or move in the slightest. They were as solid as oak boards. Carine was careful not to look down as she and Selena made their way higher than the torch tower where the wind flapped through their clothes and hair. When she glimpsed Bastion Park far below through the stairs, Carine set her jaw and continued anyway.

"What will we do at the top?" Selena asked, a few steps behind Carine.

"What I should have done from the start," Carine said. "Have you heard of Firebrand?"

"He was a sorcerer," Selena said.

"He was my granddad's master," Carine said, "and when Firebrand turned to the dark side, my granddad Jon wished for order. Order is what stopped Firebrand."

"What if the Etherrealm doesn't answer your wish?"

Carine panted, stepping up to the highest stair as her stomach sank. "I don't want to think about it."

The ceiling of Giles' new Bastion was open to the salty, Esten air. The roof was a band held up by several smooth pillars from the gardens. In the middle of the room was the throne. Around its edges were several hardback servants' chairs.

Carine's stomach wrenched. King David and Sir Alviar were shackled beside Heartless Renald, who held a staff across his chest like a weapon. David's knuckles were bloody. He and Alviar both looked worn out and drained, though not sick and dying, thank the flames. Giles, whose face bore a fresh wound, was standing tall at the top of the stairs, as though he had heard Carine and Selena coming.

When David saw Carine, he clenched his jaw, sighed, and looked away. Carine ignored him. If he wanted to hate her that was his decision. As for her, she had Esten to worry about.

"Like what I've done with the place?" Giles offered Carine and Selena a hand as they stepped into the tower. Carine ignored him. "I must say, Carine, it's impressive what you've done...completely stopping an invasion. What should we do next? I was thinking Padliot. Once Padliot comes under Navafort's reign, we'll have an enormous army. We could conquer the continent."

"*We* aren't doing anything," Carine said. "Let the king go and leave Navafort alone."

Giles lifted his eyebrow. "If that's what you want...compel me to do it."

Carine licked her lips, feeling David's, Alviar's, and Selena's eyes on her. Even though the Ember had helped her stop compelling, she knew just how easy it would be to start again.

Instead, Carine took out the *order* wishstone and placed it on her bare palm. "I'll ask you one more time: Let the king go."

Giles smiled. "It's just a matter of time before you cave. If you touch that word, it'll kill you. Go on, mispronounce. Compel. You know you crave it." Giles must have tried stopping in the past.

Carine glanced at Selena, who clutched the empty bag around her neck.

"The Healing Pools, gullon blood, and Embers...any of those will heal you," Selena told Giles.

Giles looked at Carine, surprised and a little sad. "So you've stopped compelling then? You've given up your great power."

"I'm only just embracing it." With a fierce wish to the Etherrealm, Carine closed her fingers over the glimmering Manakor word for order.

A new power pulsed through her. The floor quaked. Giles' smile evaporated.

"What are you doing?" he spat, staring at his hands. "You're interfering with my compulsion. I'm the only reason this building is standing."

Selena grabbed Carine's shoulder to keep from falling. Carine spread her feet apart and stood steady, letting *order* course through her.

David's shackles clinked as he crashed onto the floor. Alviar's hooves clopped back to maintain balance as the room swayed on its unsteady foundation.

Giles stretched out his arms, whispering madly in the Manakor tongue. He called out to maintain the integrity of the tower.

The makeshift stairs crashed stories and stories down to Bastion Park. The floor was about to cave. Looking out at the sky, Carine released the wishstone and caught herself on her knees.

Giles' magic took hold. The stairs flew back up to their place outside. The room stopped shaking. David pushed himself up onto his knee, jaw still tight and eyes holding anger. Alviar stood.

A frustrated line creased Giles' forehead as his voice rose. "Were you trying to kill us?"

Before Carine could stop him, Giles compelled the wishstone out of her hand. It sailed over the edge of the tower and fell down, down into the ocean lapping up on Esten's shores.

"There," Giles said. "Renald, arrest Carine too. And her friend. If none of you will see reason here, maybe you will in the dungeon."

Renald stepped forward with shackles.

There was nowhere to run. Carine whisked out her drawstring bag and searched for any wishstone she could find.

"If you're going to be trouble…" Giles said, compelling the bag and all the rest of Carine's hope away over the side of the tower.

Impatiently, he called forth the shackles. They bound tightly around Carine's wrists. They were made of such heavy iron that they pulled her hands down almost to the floor.

Carine's heart pounded as panic coursed through her. She shouldn't have let go of the Manakor word. This couldn't be the end. "Do the right thing, Giles."

He merely smiled. "You're in shackles. I've taken away your wishstones. How do you plan to fight me now? Are you reconsidering compulsion yourself? I highly recommend it."

As a final show of victory, Giles whispered the crown off David's head. The golden crown turned silver as it floated over to the prince.

Renald shoved Carine toward the outdoor stairs. The chains clinked as she tried not to fall. "Go back down the stairs, all of you. I'll lead you to the dungeon from there."

Carine stood up straight, but David brushed past her, his jaw set.

"She stopped compelling, your majesty," Selena pointed out.

David's back bristled, but he didn't answer. He stepped out to the stairs without a word.

Alviar nodded at Carine with compassion in the burned side of his face, then followed the king down.

Renald shoved Carine again, and she and Selena followed the king and the centaur down the steps.

"Is this it?" Carine called back to Giles, tears blurring her vision as she looked past Selena and Renald. "Is this how it ends...our friendship, your brotherhood, our kingdom?"

Giles stepped onto the top stair, watching his four prisoners descend the long tall stairway of floating objects. He didn't answer her, but stood with a smug smile, his indigo cape billowing out in the high breeze.

Carine swore under her breath.

"There is hope," Selena said, raising a comforting hand to Carine's shoulder. As she raised her arm, her sleeve revealed the glittering Manakor tattoo of *viat* on her wrist. "There is always hope."

"What?" Selena said, reacting to Carine's expression.

Carine lifted the shackles with all her might and gripped the Manakor *viat*. Selena closed her eyes and held her breath, probably wishing too.

Giles' Bastion Tower rumbled. He turned back toward the structure, as some of the stairs plummeted. Carine, Selena, David, Alviar, Renald, and Giles were still standing on floating steps, but one by one the other planks dropped. Theirs would drop soon.

"Give it up, Giles," Carine shouted, accepting the pain that tore through her.

The marble ring ceiling of his tower broke in chunks.

Giles mouthed compelling Manakor, but it wasn't enough to overpower Carine's *viat*.

"Stop wishing! We're going to fall if you don't," Renald said.

As the stairs fell beside her, she felt the wish's warm stirring and the Ember's interior silence.

*Viat.* It wasn't the word she had started with. Carine had wanted to use *order.* She had wanted to follow exactly in her granddad's footsteps. *Viat* was something else. Selena had said it was the most powerful wish. It was submission to the Etherrealm.

"I said *stop,*" Sir Renald repeated, shoving Selena off the floating board, but Carine kept hold of her wrist.

Selena shrieked. Carine was the only thing holding her up hundreds of feet over Bastion Park. The Manakor on Selena's wrist burned Carine's hand, and her arm ached as she knelt on the floating stair to keep Selena from plummeting to her death.

"Let go of the Manakor," Giles said, holding the side of his tower, which crumbled as he spoke. "I'll save Selena. Just let go of the word."

Selena begged as she swung from Carine's shackled grasp. "Don't let go. Please."

*Viat,* Carine repeated interiorly. She grunted, trying not to let go, knowing that any second her stair would fall too.

She wished for help, for order, for all to be restored better than before. She wanted Navafort to experience what she had when she received the Ember.

His Majesty King David screamed as his stair gave way.

Alviar fell next.

"Don't let go," Selena begged.

Renald and Giles' stairs gave way.

Then Carine's.

A dragon screeched.

*Viat.*

# 46

## FALLEN

One moment, Carine and Selena were in free fall. The next moment, Carine's face hit the side of Kavariel's talon as it closed over both of them.

The ash dragon swooped low with wide gorgeous wings. It snatched King David and Alviar from the air in its other talon, and lifted up, up, up.

Carine struggled to catch her breath. She released Selena's arm—Selena's head crammed against Carine's neck—as they bolted up into the clouds. Relief melted through her as fresh and bright air hit her cheeks.

"Soot and ash!" David shouted from the other talon. He peered through the dragon's claw, whooping with glee. "Alviar, look! Soot and ash…We're flying!"

Carine craned her neck to see the beast's big, fleshy underbelly. Its tail gave way to open sky, and down below, getting smaller and smaller, was Esten.

Down below, so small you could barely tell he was Giles, a silver-crowned figure looked up at the sky. He turned to the rubble and raised his arm. The tower reconstructed itself. Townsfolk crept out of hiding to see the commotion. "King" Giles raised both hands, as though he was victorious.

When the dragon passed through a white cloud, Esten disappeared.

The ash dragon Kavariel was as beautiful and mysterious from this vantage point as he had been when Carine and David had approached in his flame. Carine's heart ached, since even now in this triumphant escape, David didn't look at her, but instead exclaimed to Alviar alone what an incredible experience this was.

It occurred to her for a moment that dragons ate folk and could have snatched them up for an afternoon meal. However, after flitting through trees for what seemed at once an eternity and the blink of an eye, the dragon swooped low over some bushy trees in an unfamiliar and distant land.

Kavariel released his hold and unceremoniously dropped them into the boughs. Despite a few broken bones and bruises, they all climbed down as Kavariel soared in silhouetted circles overhead.

There was a commotion at the top of a nearby hill as several folk appeared. Carine's heart pounded as she recognized familiar faces from their journey to the healing pools—Ansa, Lord Tauno, and others—many with glittering gold Manakor on their wrists. She stood up straight, clutching her broken arm and cracking a smile. No matter what Giles had planned or how David resented her, Carine didn't care. They would get the kingdom back, and they weren't alone.

Kavariel shrieked, flapped his wings overhead, and disappeared.

# ALSO BY T.K. KISER

## THE EMBER BEARER

A Manakor Worlds Book
Coming Winter 2019
Cover and details to be announced.
Sign up for alerts at tkkiser.com

## THE MANAKOR CHRONICLES
## BOOK #3

Coming Fall 2019
Cover, title, and details to be announced.
Sign up for alerts at tkkiser.com

# THE FIREBRAND LEGACY

*The Manakor Chronicles*
*Book #1*
A magical language.
An enchanted flame.
A word to save everything.

# DEATH DRAGON'S KISS

*The Manakor Chronicles*
*Book #2*
Would you betray yourself
for someone you love?

Goodreads * Amazon * BN.com * iBooks * IndieBound

# ACKNOWLEDGEMENTS

Just as Carine would never be who she is on the last page without others, neither would this book exist without the hard work and admirable creativity of a team. I am so grateful.

Thank you to my readers, and to the schools and teachers that have embraced *The Manakor Chronicles*. It is for you I write.

Thank you to Courtney Diles Henderson and Sandra Hutchinson for your edits, and to beta readers Jasmine, Natalia, Emily, and Hayden Raines. Without your input on plot and wording, this book wouldn't be what it is. Thank you also to Kat and Bob for proofreading! It is amazing how many people can miss the same typo.

I can't rave enough about the masterful artwork of Ami Leshner. Ami, your cover illustrations visually bring Carine, the princes, Selena, and Navafort to life. Thank you.

Finally, big thanks and big hugs to my family, friends, and husband. Your support and love means the world.

AMDG,

T.K. Kiser

# ABOUT THE AUTHOR

T.K. Kiser writes fiction in Greenville, South Carolina. When she isn't writing, she researches everything, relishes good conversations, and buys too many books.

Find her online on Facebook, Instagram, and at tkkiser.com.